HEARTS IN PERIL™

Safe Haven Stalker

Sandra Orchard

Annie's®

AnniesFiction.com

Books in the Hearts in Peril series

Library of Congress-in-Publication Data
Safe Haven Stalker / by Sandra Orchard
p. cm.
ISBN: 978-1-64025-796-2
I. Title
2023935639

AnniesFiction.com
(800) 282-6643
Hearts in Peril™
Series Creator: Shari Lohner
Series Editor: Amy Woods

10 11 12 13 14 | Printed in China | 9 8 7 6 5 4 3 2 1

1

$\mathscr{A}$nnie Bishop enjoyed being in the business of restoring dreams. It helped make up for the ones she'd had to abandon.

Her young physical therapy client's eager blue eyes beamed up at her expectantly.

"You can resume playing soccer." Annie grinned at the boy's exuberant fist pump. "But keep up with the exercises I've given you. Your knee joint is hypermobile, which means it moves more than it's supposed to. Strengthening the surrounding muscles will help prevent reinjury."

Noah's aunt, Sylvie, frowned. "Are you sure it's not too soon for him to play again?"

"Ms. Annie said it's fine," the eight-year-old countered. "Dad's paranoid."

Chuckling, Annie opened the office door. "It's not too soon at all, thanks to Noah's hard work. As long as he keeps it up, he'll be fine."

She had yet to meet Noah's father, who from various comments Noah had made over the past few weeks sounded like a die-hard worrier, even more so than his aunt. Annie supposed that shouldn't surprise her. As a widower and a police officer, Noah's dad had no doubt seen more than his fair share of bad situations. Not that the small town of Safe Haven, Iowa, was a hotbed of crime. In the three months since she'd moved there from Alaska, she'd scarcely witnessed anything worse than a five-year-old swiping a lollipop from the local candy shop—definitely no mobsters.

Annie escorted Noah and his aunt to reception. "I'd like to see Noah again in two weeks, but if you have concerns in the meantime, don't hesitate to call."

"Thank you," Sylvie said. She nudged her nephew. "What do you say, Noah?"

"Thank you," the boy sang out as he skipped ahead of them, a huge difference from how he'd moved at his first appointment.

That was why Annie loved her job. Unlike her previous experience working as an ER nurse, physical therapy gave her a chance to see patients through their rehabilitation, instead of seeing them at their worst and rarely hearing how they fared afterward.

The receptionist, Debbie, handed Annie an empty folder with the name *Bernie Dyball* written on the tab. "Your next client is waiting in room C. He's new and still filling out his paperwork."

Annie bade Noah goodbye, then turned to greet her next patient.

"Ms. Bishop?" Debbie called after Annie. "I have to leave early today, so you'll need to process your last client's payment, okay?"

"I suppose I can ask Gayle for a hand if I run into trouble with the system."

"No, sorry," Debbie said. "You'll be on your own. Gayle and Ian already left."

Annie's pulse spiked. "The clinic doesn't close until five."

"They're the bosses," Debbie said. "And their appointments were finished for the day."

"I see." Annie stifled a grimace, suspecting that the receptionist hadn't asked Gayle for permission to leave early. Annie had worked with Gayle for years in Alaska before following her to Iowa. Gayle knew Annie never worked alone, especially not with an unknown male client.

Taking a deep breath, she paused outside the closed door of examination room C to allow her heart rate to settle before knocking.

When a voice inside beckoned, she let herself into the room and introduced herself.

The man, who appeared to be in his late seventies, offered her a gap-toothed smile and handed over his completed paperwork. His thinning gray hair was cropped short, his lanky posture slightly stooped.

A glance at his paperwork told her he was presenting with a shoulder complaint. "When did the pain in your shoulder start?" she asked.

"I can't remember when it didn't hurt. But my friend said you do a newfangled therapy that might give me back some mobility."

"Fascial stretch therapy, yes." Annie explained the theory behind why it often worked so well, then asked him to move his arms in several different directions. The range of motion in his left shoulder was significantly less than that of his right. "Are you left-handed?"

"Nope."

She noted it on his paperwork. "I'm going to move your limbs in progressively larger ranges to help break up scar tissue and reset your neural connections."

"Neural what?"

"The signals your body sends to your brain. When we injure ourselves, the pain we feel is a safety mechanism reminding us to limit our movement to give the injured part a chance to heal. But sometimes, long past that acute stage of injury, it keeps signaling the brain to back off."

More than one patient had teased her about needing her neural connections reset when it came to dating—a misconception she'd never bothered to correct. Annie dismissed the random thought.

"Are you saying the pain is all in my head?" Bernie sounded mildly offended. "Because it sure feels real to me."

"No, I'm saying the less you move, the more your body adapts to your new normal. And not only can that inhibit you from recovering your former range of motion, but if the restricted movement persists, you might lose even more."

He frowned. "I guess that makes sense."

"So my job is to ease your limbs back into those lost ranges. If you'll take off your sweater and lie on the massage table, we'll get started."

Bernie wore a thin T-shirt beneath the sweater, which would allow her a much better sense of the tissue movement when she targeted specific areas around his shoulder. She started with the right side, and his arm's range of motion quickly expanded under her ministrations. As she usually did while she worked, she asked Bernie questions about his interests, his hobbies, his family, and such.

Bernie was surprisingly reticent. He skirted several of her questions or repeated answers to previous questions. Perhaps he was simply a private person, but she sensed there might be more going on. He seemed to be experiencing memory lapses and working hard to cover them up.

Since older memories often came easier to senior clients, she asked him what he had done before he retired.

Bernie's shoulders tensed. "This and that," he muttered vaguely.

"Relax, please." Annie kneaded the tissue around his left shoulder joint as she moved his arm in ever-widening circles. Gnarled scar tissue, perhaps as the result of a gunshot wound or shrapnel, marred his skin below the clavicle. "Were you in the military?"

His brow furrowed. "No."

Opting not to press him for an explanation, she moved her attention away from the scar. It wasn't unusual for clients to exhibit emotional reactions when she worked on areas of former trauma. Much like the muscle memory that kicked in when performing repetitive tasks, emotional memories tended to resurface when revisiting a point of distress—memories that could complicate the resulting movement restrictions.

"Have you always lived in Safe Haven?" Annie asked.

Bernie's brow smoothed once more. "No, I found this gem eight years ago. Before that, I lived in Chicago." He tensed again.

Almost reflexively, Annie tensed too. Her hands trembled, and perspiration beaded her skin.

She'd been worried about Bernie's emotional memories, and the mere mention of Chicago had triggered hers. The city was synonymous with Joey. And she'd relived the consequences of treating Joey's bullet wound more sleepless nights than she wanted to remember. She gave her mind a mental shake. She was in Safe Haven, not Chicago. Joey's arm didn't reach that far.

"But that was a lifetime ago." Bernie's gruff tone snapped Annie back to the present.

A lifetime ago for her too. And she understood not wanting to talk about it all too well. "I moved here a few months ago, at the beginning of summer," she volunteered—something she rarely did, but in hopes that sharing a little about herself would help her new patient to relax.

He squinted at her. "You're from Chicago too?" Suspicion colored his tone.

Her heart thumped. "Uh, no. I moved here from Anchorage, Alaska." Which was the truth. *Annie Bishop* had never lived in Chicago.

Bernie scowled as if he sensed her deception. "Why the twenty questions?" he groused.

"I'm sorry. Many of my clients prefer to talk during their appointments. It keeps their minds occupied."

The appointment spiraled from bad to worse. Her experience with contrary clients usually centered on their unwillingness to do the exercises she gave them. She debated how to smooth over Bernie's growing irritation. Maybe she should stop tiptoeing around and ask him about the scar outright, like lancing a boil to rid the body of poison. Sure, her modus operandi for dealing with her own emotional trauma was to ignore, ignore, ignore, but he didn't need to know that. She edged back the collar of his T-shirt to allow a clearer view of the tissue, which was definitely a bullet wound scar. "I couldn't help noticing your scar."

Bernie Dyball jackknifed to a sitting position and swung his legs off the table.

"Wait, I merely wanted to—"

"You shouldn't have seen that." He grabbed his sweater but struggled to push his arms through the holes.

Annie reached out to assist him.

"No." He flinched away. "This was a mistake."

Sitting in the waiting room, Curt Porter recognized his son's petite physical therapist the moment she approached the reception area. With her wavy strawberry-blonde hair framing her heart-shaped face in a flattering cut, she was even more attractive in person than in her photo on the clinic's website. But her blue eyes—fixed on the fuming senior she was trailing—were troubled.

Curt stood as she moved behind the reception desk and told the man what he owed for his treatment.

Her gaze snapped to Curt, and panic flashed in her eyes. She glanced at the computer screen on the desk in front of her. "I'm sorry. Were you waiting to make an appointment?"

"I'll wait until you're finished with this gentleman." Curt smiled, hoping to ease her discomfort at his unexpected appearance. He'd been surprised to find the reception desk unoccupied and the two adjacent offices empty and dark. But he'd heard voices behind the closed door of an examination room down the hall and spotted a light in an office beyond with Ms. Bishop's name on the door, so he'd decided to bide his time until she came out.

Her hand trembled as she gave her client his change. The man immediately ambled toward the door, and Curt hurried ahead to hold it open for him.

Ms. Bishop started around the desk but then seemed to think better of it. She drew in a breath. "How may I help you Mr. . . . ?"

"Please, call me Curt."

She swallowed hard. "Curt," she repeated stiffly.

"I'm Noah's dad," he quickly added.

Sunshine dawned on her face. Coming around the desk, she extended her hand toward him. "Mr. Porter, it's so nice to meet you."

His heart kicked as he returned her handshake. He could see why his son enjoyed his physical therapy appointments. "Please, call me Curt."

"Of course. I'm Annie," she replied. "How may I help you?"

He hesitated, suddenly self-conscious over the impulse to question her judgment.

"Would you like to sit?" She motioned to the chairs in the empty waiting room, then led the way to a pair across from each other.

Following her, Curt noticed a faint hint of vanilla.

Once he settled into the seat across from her, she said, "You're concerned about Noah playing soccer again?"

He sighed. "Yes."

Her warm smile reassured him that she wasn't taking his doubts personally, but she also wasn't dismissing them out of hand. "I honestly believe Noah is more than recovered enough to play again."

"Did my sister tell you what a go-getter my son is? Noah doesn't shy away from trying to reclaim the ball from his opponents."

"I can imagine. He's been a poster child for how a client should do his physical therapy homework. The best way he can protect his knee joint is by strengthening the muscles, and he's doing a fabulous job at that. All without retriggering the pain and inflammation that he'd first presented."

Curt gave a small smile. "He was determined not to miss the fall season."

"And there's no reason why he should. But I'll tell you what. If it'll make you feel better, I'll come and watch his first game to monitor how he bears his weight as he plays. If I see anything of concern, I promise to tell you."

"That's very generous of you, but I couldn't ask you to do that."

"You didn't. I offered." Her contagious smile lit up her cornflower-blue eyes. No wonder she inspired so much confidence in Noah.

Curt ducked his head. "It would put my mind at ease, but"—he glanced at his watch—"Noah's next game starts in twenty minutes."

"No problem." Annie pushed up from her chair. "Give me a minute to jot a few notes in my last patient's file, and then I can follow you to the field."

"Great. No rush. He's playing at the community center down the road."

"I can catch up with you there if you'd prefer."

"I'm happy to wait. I'm not sure offhand which of the three fields he'll be on."

"I'll be back in a few minutes." She flashed that bright smile once more and disappeared into her office.

A guy could almost look forward to getting injured if he knew she'd be his therapist.

A few minutes later, she returned, keys in hand, and he waited in the building's main lobby while she locked the clinic doors. Rejoining him, she said, "I drive the blue sedan in the back corner of the parking lot. Where are you parked?"

"A couple of cars away." He held the door open for her, then strode along by her side toward their cars. The warm September air held the promise of a beautiful evening. Curt paused at his car to wait for Annie to reach hers. But, noticing a dark puddle beneath her car, he hurried after her. "Wait. Your car has a leak."

Leaning down, Annie frowned at the puddle. "Can you tell what it is?"

Using the flashlight on his cell phone, Curt reached under the car far enough to smear a bit of the fluid between his fingers and survey the area directly above the puddle. "Bad news, I'm afraid. I think that's a leak in your brake line. I'll call Mick's Garage for a tow."

"I know Mick. He's the mechanic who checked the car over before I bought it, used."

"He's good and doesn't overcharge. With any luck he can replace the line while you watch Noah's game. Then I can drive you to the garage to pick it up afterward."

"That would be great. Thanks. But I can wait here for Mick and then jog over to the community center. I don't want you to miss the start of Noah's game."

Curt didn't want to admit his son wasn't expecting him. As a police officer, he couldn't take off a couple of hours whenever his son had a game. Noah understood that. Curt dropped by the games when he could, or when he had the day off, but the rest of the time, he depended on Sylvie to get Noah to and from the games and to be his cheering section. But when his sister had called an hour before to tell Curt that the physical therapist had given Noah the green light to resume playing, Curt had asked Officer Young if she would come in early to cover the end of his shift.

Mick showed up with his tow truck within minutes of Curt's call, and Annie and Curt made it to the soccer field in time for the kickoff.

Noah spotted Curt the minute they arrived, and his grin widened when he saw Annie.

"What brings you here?" Sylvie asked Annie.

"I told Curt I'd watch Noah's first game to make sure he's not overtaxing his knee."

Sylvie crossed her arms. "I thought you were confident he's strong enough to play."

"I am, but I got the sense his dad needed a little hand-holding yet." She winked at Curt.

He chuckled, trying to ignore the way his heart kicked at the pleasant image she'd conjured. "I took the rest of the day off," he told his sister. "So if you have other things you want to get done, I can take over here."

Sylvie's gaze darted between him and Annie. "I'd kind of like to see the game."

He smiled. She was the best sister a brother could ask for, and as dedicated as he was about watching out for Noah.

Curt and Annie raced up and down the sideline cheering Noah on. And when he scored the first goal of the game, Annie threw Curt a high five.

Wow, this is a lot of fun. He definitely had to try to get to more of Noah's games.

Annie beamed. "I haven't had this much fun in years."

"Yeah." Watching her enthusiasm was almost as much fun as watching Noah play.

His cell phone rang and for a moment, he contemplated ignoring it until he glanced at the screen. "Hey, Mick. Is there a problem?"

"I'd say so." Mick's usual jovial tone was conspicuously absent. "How well do you know Annie Bishop?"

"Why?"

"Because someone doesn't like her much."

Curt's pulse quickened. "What do you mean?"

"Her brake line was cut."

It can't be starting again. Annie blinked back tears. She'd changed names, careers, and states. He couldn't have found her. She fixed her attention on the young players racing down the soccer field. *He couldn't have.*

"Annie?" Curt's concerned baritone cut into her thoughts.

Hugging herself, she tried to make eye contact, but couldn't quite manage it.

"Has someone threatened you?" He stood over six feet, and every muscle in his body seemed primed to defend her.

She bit her lip to stop its quivering. The cop who'd told her to leave Chicago had warned her that a restraining order against Joey would make his attentions become ugly. Had disappearing done the same?

"Annie?" Curt pressed.

The cop's warning echoed through her mind. *Guys like Joey have too many minions on the inside—cops or judges who can be blackmailed, because anyone with loved ones or a career they care about can be coerced into doing his bidding.*

Annie watched Noah on the soccer field. Tamping down her rising panic, she said firmly, "No. I moved here three months ago. I've scarcely had time to get to know anyone, never mind make enemies."

Curt caught her arm, his gentle grasp warm and reassuring. "It'll all work out." He dipped his head until she met his gaze. His brown eyes simmered with concern. "We'll figure this out. Okay?"

Not trusting her voice, she simply nodded.

Curt's sister touched his arm. "I'm heading out."

"See you later, Sylv. Thanks for everything." To Annie, he said, "Our perpetrator might have mistaken your car for his intended target."

Our perpetrator? His solidarity was oddly comforting but also unnerving. "My name is on a sign in front of the parking space," she protested.

"Once you park, those signs aren't that visible."

Annie blew out a long slow breath. That was true. She shivered. "Still, the fact that anyone in Safe Haven would cut someone's brake lines doesn't make me feel much better."

"Mick could be wrong. I asked him not to touch anything else until I can see the line for myself. I'll drive you home after the game, then go straight to his shop."

She swallowed the fear balling in her throat. "Thanks." She lived about a mile and a half away and could easily walk, but that would make her a really easy target.

"We've had a few mischief complaints the past couple of weeks. Benign stuff like toilet-papering the trees in the gym teacher's front yard or flipping the street signs. The kind of dares teenagers pull. The pranks may have escalated."

"That's kind of a serious escalation."

"Yeah. We do have a boy in town who struggles to foresee the potential consequences of his actions, which makes him an easy mark for other kids' dares. I'll talk to him."

The referee blew the whistle to signal the end of the game, and Noah dashed toward Annie and his dad. "Ms. Annie, did you see my goal?"

"I sure did. Great job." She jutted her chin toward his leg. "How's the knee feel?"

"Doesn't hurt at all."

She grinned, pretty sure he wouldn't admit it if it did.

Curt gave his son a one-armed hug. "Way to play, Champ."

Noah lit up at his father's praise, and Annie's heart stirred. Noah clearly adored his father. "You got a son playing in the game too, Ms. Annie?" Noah asked.

"No, I came to see you play. To make sure you didn't push that knee of yours too far." She winked.

"Wasn't that nice of her?" Curt chimed in.

"Yeah, I told you she was nice." Noah grinned up at his dad.

"That you did." A dimple dented Curt's left cheek and the corners of his eyes crinkled attractively when he smiled.

Annie's face heated, and she averted her gaze. She usually made a point of *not* noticing a guy's smile. No attachments meant criminals like Joey had no leverage to use against her.

Noah tugged on his dad's sleeve. "We should take Ms. Annie for an ice cream to thank her, don't you think?"

Curt burst into laughter—a joyous, carefree sound that momentarily pushed the specter of Joey from her thoughts. "How can you argue with that logic?" Curt sounded as if he loved his son's idea.

"As lovely as that sounds," Annie agreed, "could I take a rain check? I have a dog at home, and she'll be wondering what's keeping me so late."

"Can I meet her?" Noah begged.

"Of course."

"We're bringing Ms. Annie home," his dad explained. "She had car trouble. Then we'll stop by Mick's Garage on our way home."

"Where's Aunt Sylvie?" Noah asked.

"I told her I'd pick you up."

"Awesome." Noah slipped his hand into Annie's.

She shot Curt a startled glance, but he didn't seem bothered by his son's lack of reserve. Not that Annie minded either, if she were honest.

Noah's affability was endearing. On the short drive to her house, he kept up a lively conversation about the game and his coach and the new jerseys they'd ordered.

The boy was a bundle of energy.

Curt steered onto her street. "Which house?"

"Twenty-three. On the left. I'm renting from Grace Kemp."

"Right." Curt slowed the car. "I remember Sylvie mentioning that."

"You two know Grace?"

"Grandma Grace?" Noah piped up. "She makes the best chocolate chip cookies for our kids' club at church."

"As you can see, my son has a food fixation," Curt said.

"Don't all growing boys?" She laughed. As Curt pulled into her driveway, a disturbing thought niggled at Annie. She lowered her voice. "I just thought of one person in Safe Haven who might have a grudge against me."

Curt's expression sobered. "Who's that?"

"Grace's former tenant. He didn't want to leave. But Grace opted not to renew his lease at the end of the summer so she could let the place to me. I moved here to work for her son and daughter-in-law at the clinic, and with the dog to accommodate, none of the vacant apartments in town were a viable option." She took in the small bungalow and winced. "When I accepted her offer, I didn't realize Grace was ousting the existing tenant for my sake."

"You have nothing to apologize for. Do you know the tenant's name?"

"No. Sorry."

"Not a problem. I'll ask Grace. And I'll get back to you as soon as I know more."

She thanked him and climbed out of the car, then cocked her ear at the sound of Bella's distinctive howl. "That's weird."

"What?"

"That sounded like it came from the backyard, but I always leave my dog locked in the house when I'm at work."

Curt hopped out of the car and directed Noah to stay put.

"But Annie said I could see her dog," Noah whined from the back seat.

"Maybe another time," Curt admonished, radiating tension.

Curt's senses shifted into high alert. "Given what happened with your brakes, we shouldn't assume anything." He caught a glimpse of Noah in the back seat, wishing he hadn't sent Sylvie home early. "If you give me your house keys, I can ensure no one's inside. I need you to stay here with Noah. All right?"

Annie's eyes widened. He hated to worry her unduly, but until he scouted the premises, he couldn't know if there was cause for concern.

"How about I take Noah into the backyard to meet Bella?" Annie suggested. "Otherwise, he's going to ask a lot of questions and might get scared watching you skulk about."

Curt gritted his teeth. "You're right. But I'll check the yard first. Is Bella aggressive?"

"No, but she is an enthusiastic greeter." Annie rummaged through her bag and then handed him a packet of dog treats. "Offer her one of these, and she should sit instead of jumping all over you."

Relieved the dog would allow him into the yard, Curt palmed a treat and tucked the bag into his pocket. But for Annie's protection, he wished Bella weren't so easy to befriend.

The dog became increasingly vocal as Curt unlatched the six-foot wooden gate. "Hey, Bella," he called, pushing open the gate. "I have a treat for you."

The sleek gray-and-white husky promptly sat in front of him, her tail swishing over the grass.

"Good girl." He tossed her the treat, and she caught it midair. "Your mom will be here in a minute." Curt scanned the fenced yard. "Is there anyone here we should know about?" Aside from the shed in the back corner, there was no place to hide. He stalked along the rear of the house, checking each window for evidence of a break-in.

Bella trailed him, alternating between sniffing his footsteps and the pocket that held the treat bag. The windows and back door were all securely locked.

Curt circled the shed, tested the padlock—which was shut tight—and peeked through a small window in the door. "All clear here." He tossed the dog another treat.

Rounding the house, he signaled to Annie, who'd joined Noah in the back seat. Noah burst from the car ahead of her. "Is Bella okay?"

"She's fine. Annie will introduce you. I need to go inside for a minute."

Annie passed him her keys. The graze of her cool, trembling fingers betrayed her fear.

He squeezed her hand reassuringly. "Everything is secure at the back of the house."

To his surprise, she frowned.

"What's wrong?"

She winced. "When I let Bella out in the morning, I don't lock the door. So, if I forgot to let her in before I left, the door should still have been unlocked. I suppose I must've locked it, thinking I'd already let her in. I can't tell if that's good or bad."

Her obvious apprehension, despite the brave face she attempted to present, reinforced his suspicion that she'd held back when he first questioned her. The question was why? If he didn't know better, he'd think she was covering for an abusive husband. Then again, for all he knew she could have an abusive husband or ex-boyfriend in her past.

Curt fisted his hand until the keys dug into his palm. "I'll check inside." He let himself in through the back door and cleared each room one at a time, including the basement. The place was bright and airy in pastel colors, sparsely furnished but with a homey feel that was enhanced by the lingering aroma of baked bread. Gorgeous scenic photographs of Alaska decorated the walls of the living room.

From what he could see, there was no evidence of a man in her life, past or present. If she'd had a significant other, she didn't appear to have included him in her new life in Safe Haven.

Curt rejoined Annie and Noah outside. "Everything's locked up tight. No sign of an intruder." Another possibility occurred to him. "Do you have Grace's number on you?"

Annie pulled out her cell phone. "Yes. Why?"

"Give her a call and ask if she sent her handyman over to do repairs."

Annie shrank back. "I'd rather not. If she didn't, it'll upset her. I'm sure I must have forgotten to let Bella back in this morning."

Curt hid a grimace, not wanting to force the issue. "If you talk to her later, perhaps you could casually bring it up."

"Sure, I'll try."

He searched her gaze. "Can you think of anything else I should know? Anything that might help me track down who tampered with your car, I mean."

Hugging herself, she shook her head. "No. I think it's like you said. A case of mistaken identity."

"Dad, watch this," Noah called. He told the dog to sit, then stay, then paced a few feet away.

"Impressive," Curt said to Annie, who was standing beside him.

Noah returned to Bella and held up a hand. "High five."

Bella raised a paw and tapped it against Noah's open palm.

"Wow, that's great."

Noah whooped and gave Bella a treat and a hug.

Curt grinned at Annie. "That's quite the dog you have there."

She chuckled. "The winter nights are very long in Alaska. They gave me lots of time to teach her tricks."

"Ah, you're from Alaska. That explains the gorgeous photos in your living room."

Her cheeks grew rosy. "It's easy to be a good photographer when you have those scenic views for inspiration."

"Iowa is a long way from Alaska. What brought you to Safe Haven?"

She visibly relaxed, and her infectious smile returned to her lips. "I worked with Gayle and Ian at their clinic in Anchorage. But after they moved back here to be close to Grace, I didn't get along with the Alaska clinic's new owner. When Gayle heard about it, she invited me to join them at their clinic here."

"That must be a big change for you. Or do you have family here too?"

"No. I didn't know anyone here besides Gayle and Ian. But that's okay. Everyone is very nice. Grace has practically adopted me."

"She's a sweetheart. Where's your family? Back in Alaska?"

"No, I lost my parents a number of years ago and have no siblings."

"I'm sorry." Curt didn't know what he would've done without his sister's support after his wife died.

Annie's smile dimmed. "Thank you."

"Do you have someone who can give you a lift to work tomorrow? Mick probably won't have your car ready before midday."

"I don't schedule appointments on Saturdays. But even if I had to go in, it's close enough for me to walk or ride my bike—something I would like to do more often anyway."

Curt chuckled. "I'm sure your rambunctious dog prefers you save your walks for her."

"That's so true. I take her out every evening, sometimes in the morning before work, when I have time, and I give her extra-long walks on the weekends."

Bella's ears pricked up.

"I see she knows the magic word."

Annie smiled at her dog. "Yup, there's no fooling her. She even knows how to spell it."

Curt raised his eyebrows. "You mean to tell me that if I asked if you were going to take her for a w-a-l-k, she'd know what I was saying?"

Bella yipped and trotted over to join them.

Annie laughed. "Now you've done it."

Curt gaped at the animal. "She seemed totally focused on Noah. I can't believe she picked up on my spelling."

"It is her favorite thing." Annie winked at Noah.

"Say goodbye to Bella," Curt said to his son. "We need to go." He pressed a business card into Annie's hand. "Call me if you think of anything that might aid my investigation, or if anything else of concern occurs."

Studying the card, she rubbed it between her fingers, as if suddenly reluctant to meet his gaze.

There was no doubt about it. Annie Bishop was hiding something.

3

*A*nnie dragged herself off the sofa and searched for her ringing phone. She'd jumped at every shadow while walking Bella and then hadn't had the energy to do more than heat up a frozen pizza for supper. She pressed her fingertips to her temples, trying to soothe her throbbing head. She hadn't had such a headache since the first few months after she fled Chicago and Joey's unwelcome attentions.

She shuddered. Clearly the possibility that he'd found her had retriggered the pain.

If not for Curt's assurance that her house hadn't been broken into, she might've never settled down. She dreaded to think what might have happened if he hadn't noticed the puddle of brake fluid under her car. The man had served as her guardian angel all day.

She wished she didn't feel so guilty about not mentioning Joey to Curt. She wanted to trust him, but the Chicago detective had warned her against trusting law enforcement. And given how overprotective Curt was of his son, Joey would only have to threaten Noah's well-being to win Curt's cooperation.

Spotting the phone on the kitchen counter, she snatched it up on the last ring before it would have gone to voice mail. "Hey, Grace, how are you doing?" Like Annie had told Curt, Grace was more than a landlady to her. She'd opened her guest room to Annie until the former tenant's lease on the place had expired.

Annie's pulse rippled. Could Grace's previous renter have lashed out at her over not receiving an offer to renew his lease?

"I'm good," Grace said, her voice void of its usual cheery timbre. "But I received a strange call from Officer Curt Porter. Do you know him?"

Annie squirmed. "Uh, yes, I met him today. He's the father of a client." How could Curt go behind her back and question Grace?

"He said you had car trouble today?" Her inflection invited Annie to elaborate.

Muffling a groan, Annie rubbed her fingertip through a minuscule layer of dust on the kitchen counter. "Yes, but no harm done. Mick should have it fixed tomorrow."

"Curt said the damage wasn't accidental and asked me about my previous tenant." A hint of sternness crept into her voice. "I really don't think he'd hold a grudge against you, dear. Granted, his behavior sometimes strikes folks as different, but that's because he is neurodiverse. He has autism." Her tone was protective. "But he's a kind young man."

Annie sank onto the stool next to the counter and rested her head in her hand. "I'm sure he is." And if she'd known before what Grace had just shared with her, she would have refused to take the place from him, no matter what. Finding a new place to live was stressful for anyone, but adapting to a whole change in routine was particularly stressful for someone with autism. "I'm sorry for mentioning him to Cur—uh, Officer Porter. I told him I hadn't lived here long enough to make any enemies."

"I can't imagine anyone wanting to hurt you," Grace said warmly. "You're one of the sweetest people I know."

The warmth in Grace's voice soothed Annie's frayed nerves. "Thank you."

"Are you okay, dear? You don't sound well."

Annie straightened. "Fighting a headache, I'm afraid."

"Have you had the furnace on? There was a news report tonight about a family who almost died from carbon monoxide poisoning due to a blocked chimney. A headache is one of the first symptoms."

"I'm sure it's stress. The furnace has been on at night for the past week already. I'm sure I would've noticed symptoms before now if that were the problem." Not to mention the carbon monoxide detector in the hallway would have gone off. Grace was careful to maintain a safe home for her tenants.

"I'm sure you're right. Besides, I had a high-efficiency furnace put in there a few years ago, so it doesn't even have a chimney. And my handyman serviced it right before you moved in."

Feeling guilty about suspecting Curt of going around her to ask Grace about the handyman, Annie feigned a nonchalant tone and said, "Your handyman didn't happen to come by today, did he?"

"No. Did you need something repaired?"

Annie's stomach twisted. "Not at all. Everything is good."

"He'll probably be over to mow the lawn a time or two yet. And to clean the gutters. Otherwise, he won't be by again until spring unless we alert him to a problem."

"Good to know. Thanks."

"I'd better let you go, dear. You should relax in a warm bath and then get some sleep."

Annie agreed and thanked her for calling. Gratitude warred with fear that Curt was taking her tampered brakes so seriously. Why were such things happening to her? Surely Joey would've moved on to some other obsession after so many years.

The warmth of Noah's hand clasping hers pushed into her thoughts, followed by the high five she'd shared with Curt over the boy's goal. For a few minutes on the field that afternoon, she'd felt like a normal person. It had been nice. Really nice. But such attachments were exactly what she had to avoid if she wanted to ensure Joey never had the power to control her. She pushed to her feet and headed toward the bathroom. "You want to go outside before I have a bath?" she asked Bella.

Bella grunted without lifting her head.

"Okay, then." Annie flipped the hall light switch, but the light didn't come on. Pressing her palm to her throbbing head, she squinted at the ceiling fixture. She'd need a ladder to change the light bulb. It could wait until tomorrow. She tromped toward the bathroom in the semidarkness and noticed that the carbon monoxide detector plugged into the hall outlet didn't have a green light glowing. Maybe the breaker feeding the two circuits had blown. But the CO detector should have had a backup battery. She unplugged the detector and removed the battery cover. The compartment was empty.

That was weird, because every CO detector she'd ever owned had beeped annoyingly whenever the battery was low or missing, which might explain why the former tenant could have powered off the breaker. Except she was sure she'd used the hall light since moving in.

Grace's story about the family poisoned by carbon monoxide whispered through Annie's thoughts. "Better safe than sorry," she muttered to Bella, patting the dog's head as she trekked downstairs to check the breaker panel in the far corner of the basement.

At the bottom of the stairs, a chill shivered through her, and she hesitated. She was overthinking. She'd let that afternoon's episode with her car foment her imagination. Because aside from a few boxes she had yet to unpack and a basket of dirty laundry waiting to be washed, the basement was virtually empty. Nothing appeared out of place.

She sniffed the air and caught a whiff of sandalwood, the fragrance of choice of the previous tenant—a preference she'd deduced the day she moved in, based on the strong smell in the bathroom cupboard.

"Must be the furnace moving old air," she said to herself, rolling her eyes. Drawing a fortifying breath, she padded to the breaker panel. Sure enough, one of the breakers was open. She closed it and the instant blare of the CO monitor made her jump. She raced upstairs two at a time. Bella paced at the top, whining unhappily. "I'm sorry, Bella. I should have remembered to leave the detector unplugged until I replace the battery."

Holding her palms over her ears to dull the shriek of the detector, she hurried to the hall and yanked it out of the outlet, only mentally processing the code she'd glimpsed on the screen after the device fell silent. "Wait—that wasn't the code for a dead battery." She plugged the detector back in and winced. The screen informed her that significant CO levels had been detected.

She ran to the kitchen and pushed open a window, then grabbed her phone and snapped on Bella's leash. "We've got to get out of here."

She shoved open a living room window on her way past and yanked open the front door. Bella burst out ahead of her and didn't stop until she'd tugged Annie off the porch and halfway down the driveway.

Down the street, a dark sedan roared to life.

"Sorry to bother you at home," Curt's colleague said when Curt answered the phone. "I thought you'd want to know the fire department just got a 911 call for a possible carbon monoxide leak at Annie Bishop's."

Curt's heart slammed into his ribs. "Is she conscious?"

"Yes. She made the call. She's the woman whose brakes were cut, right?"

"Yes. Thanks for the heads-up. I'll go right over. Has an ambulance been dispatched?"

"Affirmative."

Curt called his sister, who lived next door, and asked her to stay with Noah since his son was already in bed for the night.

Five minutes later, at the sound of a car pulling into the driveway, he glanced out the window. It was Sylvie next door. She climbed out of her car and carried a grocery sack into her house. Two minutes later, she let herself in his front door. "I thought you were supposed to be off this weekend. What's going on?"

"New development in the Annie Bishop case." Curt stuffed his reloaded gun into his shoulder holster.

"And the officer on duty can't handle it?" Sylvie sounded perturbed.

"Did you have other plans for the evening? Because I could call—"

"No, it's not that. It's fine. But make sure you don't back out on tomorrow's trip to the orchard and pumpkin patch. Noah has been talking about it all week."

"I won't." He gave his sister's shoulder a quick squeeze. "Thanks. You're the best."

He sped across town to Annie's place. Why hadn't she called him? He'd given her his number, and a house filling with carbon monoxide kind of topped the list of suspicious occurrences. He slapped his palm against the steering wheel. He must have missed something when he searched her place.

A fire truck blocked Annie's street. Curt parked several houses away and raced toward the ambulance. He skidded to a stop at its yawning doors, but the vehicle was empty. He caught the arm of a passing paramedic. "Where's Annie? The owner of the house."

"They haven't found her yet."

Curt's pulse quickened. Spotting the fire chief heading into the house, Curt intercepted him. "Is Annie still in there? Dispatch told me she made the call."

Chief Hartwell grimaced. "Windows and doors were wide open when we got here. But there's no sign of the occupant. An officer is checking with the neighbors." He continued into the house.

Curt swallowed down his panic. Going to her neighbor's made sense. "One more thing," he called after the chief. "Have you found the source of the gas yet?"

"That was the easy part." Hartwell paused in the entranceway. "The furnace is the only fuel-burning appliance in the place, but we haven't figured out where the leak is. For now, we've turned it off."

"There's no evidence of tampering?"

"Tampering?" The chief cocked his head. "You think this could be deliberate?"

"Maybe." Curt watched the neighborhood gawkers, any one of whom could be there to admire their handiwork. "Earlier today, Ms. Bishop's brakes were cut." He lowered his voice. "But we have no idea who cut them, or why."

The chief whistled. "Okay, I'll have a guy go through every inch of the furnace from top to bottom."

"Any chance you can get him here tonight?" Curt asked. "If this was foul play, it's the second attempt on Ms. Bishop's life in less than six hours. We can't afford to give whoever is behind it all another six."

"I hear you. I'll get Phil here right away."

"Great." Phil was the owner of Phil's Furnace Repair, a mainstay of Safe Haven for more than twenty years. If anyone could ferret out the cause of the CO leak, it was him. "Keep me posted." Curt started back toward the street.

Officer Young, their newest part-time recruit, stepped off a neighbor's porch and flagged him down.

Curt jogged across the street. "Is Annie inside?"

"No. I haven't found anyone who's seen her yet. Mr. Jones"—Young motioned to the house she'd exited—"said he heard car tires squeal. Unfortunately, by the time he glanced out the window, he was too late to see the car, but he saw Annie's husky racing down the street."

Curt's gut clenched. He shouldn't have left her alone. He'd sensed there was more going on than she'd admitted. He should have stayed and pushed her into telling him everything. And his hope that the brake tampering was nothing more than an ill-advised teenage dare had been dashed when he learned that the class with the most troublemakers had been out of town on a field trip that day and hadn't returned to Safe Haven until six. "Talk to all these people standing around," Curt instructed Officer Young. "Ask if any of them saw the car. I'll issue a BOLO for Annie and her dog."

As Curt got off the phone with dispatch, Phil's repair truck rumbled up the street, maneuvering around the emergency vehicles. Every fiber in Curt's being wanted to be out searching for Annie, but with no idea who'd taken her—if she had even been abducted—his best chance of finding a lead was there at her house. He grabbed his fingerprint kit from the trunk and joined Phil. "I need to dust the furnace for fingerprints before you get started, in case we're dealing with sabotage."

"Have you checked the exhaust pipe? Stuffing that would be the simplest way to cause a carbon monoxide buildup in the house," Phil said.

Was it really that simple? Curt gritted his teeth. He should have thought to check the exhaust pipe when he was checking the house earlier.

They walked to the back of the house, and Phil shone his flashlight into the exhaust pipe opening. "There's nothing obvious. I'll need to put a vacuum on it or run a plumbing snake through to be sure."

"Okay." Curt dusted the outside of the pipe for prints and secured a couple of complete ones. Inside, he lifted several more prints from the furnace panels. Then, satisfied he'd done all he could for the time being, he gave Phil the all clear to begin his inspection and handed over his business card. "Call if you find anything."

Phil tucked the card into his shirt pocket. "Will do."

Curt went in search of the fire chief once more. Outside, he found that the ambulance had already left on another call and the volunteer firefighters were climbing back on their rig to return to the station. "Chief Hartwell, hold up a minute. I need elimination prints from any of your crew who touched the furnace or its exhaust pipe."

Hartwell turned to his team. "Anyone touch either of those?"

A chorus of negative responses came back.

"Then you just need the furnace inspector's fingerprints," Hartwell said.

"Where can I find him?"

"He went for a plumber's snake. Should be back soon."

Curt's phone rang. Glancing at the screen, he excused himself to answer. "Did they find her?"

"No."

His heart rampaged.

"But we have a report of a howling coyote scrabbling about in someone's backyard like it's caught on something and can't get away."

"Why are you bothering me with nuisance calls?" Curt's hand fisted around his phone. "I'm not even supposed to be on duty. The priority is finding Annie Bishop."

"Hear me out," the dispatcher said. "I've seen Bishop's husky at the dog park before when I've been out jogging. It's a sleek dog. Someone could easily mistake it for a coyote in the dark. And if she ran away dragging a leash, the leash could have gotten caught on something in the caller's yard, which might explain why the dog's howling instead of leaving."

Curt hurried toward his car. "Give me the address. I'll check it out."

The dispatcher rattled off an address four blocks away. "Do you want me to call animal control too?"

Curt patted the pocket where he'd stuffed the bag of treats Annie had given him earlier. "Hold off for now. I met the dog earlier today, so I should be able to take care of it. Update Officer Young on where I'm going." He started his car and as he pulled a U-turn, his headlights swept over something dark and fuzzy lying in the street next to the curb. Curt stomped on the brakes, shoved the car into park, and hopped out of the vehicle. At the sight of a fluffy purple slipper, Curt dropped to his knees.

He'd seen the same slippers in Annie's house.

A secondary crime scene? He resisted the impulse to snatch up the slipper. But a tuft of white dog fur clinging to the purple fluff clinched his fear that the slipper belonged to Annie. A wave of nausea crashed over him.

Officer Young raced up to him. "What's going on? Dispatch said—"

Curt surged to his feet. "That's Annie Bishop's slipper. And until we know how she lost it, we need to treat this as a possible crime scene. I want you to cordon this off." He squinted at the house opposite. "Have you talked to those people yet?"

"No."

"Do it now. Maybe they saw what happened here." Blinded by visions of Annie running for her life from some crazed ex-boyfriend, or worse, Curt struggled to maintain control. "There's got to be a reason why she didn't stop to put her slipper back on."

None of which could be good.

$\mathcal{D}$arkness shrouded Annie as awareness slowly returned. She didn't recognize the voices coming from somewhere above, and panic sliced through her. She squeezed her eyes tighter. They couldn't know she was awake. Not yet. Not until she had a plan. She took stock of her situation. Her head throbbed and dampness seeped through the back of her shirt. The air smelled of fresh-cut grass. Was she lying on a lawn?

"Will she be okay?" a woman asked, concern vibrating in her voice.

Not Joey's voice. Why had she feared it would be? Annie slowly opened her eyes and blinked at the dim light, still too disoriented to recognize where she was or remember how she got there. She blinked again, and a man came into focus above her.

She jerked into a sitting position but immediately swayed from dizziness. She braced her hands behind her, and the grass twined between her fingers.

"Don't try to get up," the man ordered.

Locking gazes with him, Annie scrabbled backward on her hands and feet, in just her socks. Where were her shoes? She bumped into something prickly.

"Whoa there," the man said. "I won't hurt you. My name's Tom. I'm here to help."

Tom. She didn't know anyone by that name. Annie glanced behind her and saw that she'd backed into a hedge. She could hear Bella howling in the distance. "What have you done with my dog?"

"Nothing. I'm a paramedic. You collapsed on this woman's lawn, and she called an ambulance."

A kind-faced woman drifted into Annie's field of vision and smiled down at her. "Were you trying to catch your dog?"

The memories flooded back. "Yes. Yes, I remember now." Annie pressed her palm to the side of her head. "Why does my head hurt so much?"

"Maybe you hit it when you fell," the woman speculated.

"Let's get you off this damp ground and onto a gurney," the paramedic said gently. "Then we can check you over and see if we can figure out what happened. Do you remember your name?"

"Annie Bishop."

Tom chuckled. "Mystery solved."

"Huh?"

"You called 911 because of a carbon monoxide leak. When we couldn't find you at the house, the police went door-to-door searching for you."

A second man maneuvering a gurney next to her said, "I'll report in so they can call off the BOLO."

Tom clipped an oximeter onto her finger. "If you inhaled too much CO before you got out of the house, it could explain your headache and why you lost consciousness after exerting yourself chasing your dog."

"Bella ran after a car, and I lost hold of her lead," Annie recalled.

"I'm sure the cops will secure your dog," Tom reassured, as he and his partner carefully lifted her onto the gurney. "We're going to wheel you into the ambulance so we have better light to check you over. Then we can decide if you need to go to the hospital."

She bit her lip but didn't argue.

Tom checked her oximeter reading and affixed an oxygen mask over her mouth. "Your level is a little low. This should help clear your head." He took her blood pressure. "From the sounds of those howls, one of your neighbors has caught your dog and probably already called the authorities."

"I'll walk down the street and see if I can pinpoint where she is," the woman offered from the door of the ambulance.

Annie pulled the oxygen mask down enough to be heard and lifted her head to see the woman. "Would you?"

"Of course. No need for you to worry about your dog on top of your other troubles." The woman reached in and patted Annie's foot reassuringly. "I'll be back in a jiff."

From the woman's white hair and deep smile lines, she looked to be in her seventies. "Bella likes to pull on the lead," Annie cautioned, "but if you tell her to heel, she should listen."

Tom plunked the mask back into position. "No more talking."

"Don't worry. We'll manage," the woman said confidently.

Tires squealed, a car door slammed, and the sound of pounding footfalls drew closer.

Annie clung to the sides of the gurney, every muscle tense. The image of the dark sedan speeding away from her house flashed through her mind. *Joey?* Surely, he wouldn't confront her in front of witnesses.

Curt skidded into view. "How bad is she?"

At his anguished question, Annie relaxed her stranglehold on the sides of the gurney, and the fear washed out of her body.

At the sight of Annie's bright eyes locking with his over her oxygen mask, Curt drew in his first full breath since finding her abandoned slipper on the street.

"She seems to be recovering quickly," the paramedic said. "I doubt she'll need to go into a hyperbaric chamber. I suspect the exertion of chasing her dog combined with the mildly depleted oxygen levels caused her to pass out. They might want to monitor her for a couple of hours at the hospital though."

Annie shook her head and tried to talk through the mask. She pulled it from her face. "I can't leave Bella."

"The woman who called us has gone down the street to see if she can locate the dog," the paramedic interjected, replacing Annie's oxygen mask. "Ms. Bishop recognized the dog's howl, and she didn't sound far away."

"Yeah, we got a call about her." Curt reached into the ambulance and squeezed Annie's knee. "I can hang onto Bella until you're released." A dozen questions raced through his mind, but she needed to keep the oxygen mask in place. "I'm glad you're okay. While the paramedics finish checking you over, I'll see about finding your dog."

A block away, Curt found a spry senior walking a tongue-lolling Bella. The dog must have recognized him, because she gave a yip and tugged on her leash when she saw him.

"Heel," the woman commanded, and Bella settled.

"Good evening." He displayed his badge. "I'm Officer Porter. Are you the one who called the ambulance?"

"That's right. Maxine Jenkins. The poor young woman dodged a car racing across the road. I thought for sure he would hit her, but she made it across, and then she keeled over on my front lawn."

Curt's pulse quickened. "Did the car seem to be chasing her?"

Maxine frowned. "I don't think so. She was calling her dog." She leaned down and scratched Bella on the back of the neck. "This one's a runner. Aren't you, you naughty girl?"

Bella wagged her tail.

"I can take her now if you'd like," Curt volunteered.

"Yes, I suppose that's best."

Curt returned to the ambulance, giving credit to the good Samaritan for finding Bella.

One of the paramedics climbed from the back of the rig and took a seat behind the steering wheel.

"Can I ask her a few questions before you leave?" Curt asked the paramedic who remained at Annie's side.

The man moved out of Curt's way. "Make it short and keep the oxygen mask in place as much as possible."

Curt gave him Bella's leash to hold and squatted beside the gurney.

Annie's doleful eyes met his as she pulled her mask down a bit. "I'm sorry I didn't call. As soon as the detector went off, I ran out of the house so fast I left your card behind."

"You did the right thing, hightailing it out of there." But if she'd exited immediately, she shouldn't have inhaled enough CO to need to go to the hospital. He furrowed his brow. Her account didn't add up. "Where is your CO detector?"

"In the hall outside the bedrooms. But it wasn't powered at first. The breaker was off."

"That shouldn't have mattered. The monitors have a battery backup."

"The battery compartment was empty when I checked."

Curt clenched his fist. He'd have to go back to the house and dust the monitor and breaker panel for prints. "Did you notice anything out of place we should know about? Or see anyone lurking about?"

She shook her head.

"A neighbor mentioned hearing car tires squeal away and seeing your dog racing down the street," he explained.

"Yes, when I ran out of the house, a dark sedan sped off. Bella chased after it." Her hand trembled as she pushed her oxygen mask back into place.

"Did you happen to notice the make, model, or color of the car, or glimpse who was driving?"

She spoke around the mask. "It was a four-door, I think. Maybe dark gray or blue, not quite black."

"I'll talk to the neighbors and find out who had any guests over tonight."

"Good to go?" the paramedic asked from the doorway.

"Sure." Curt pulled a new business card from his wallet and pressed it into Annie's hand. "Have the nurse call me if you need anything. As soon as inspections are finished at your place, I'll come by the hospital. Is that all right?"

Gratitude gleamed in her eyes.

Curt reclaimed Bella, and the two of them hopped down from the ambulance.

As it drove away, Bella whined. "Don't worry, girl. She'll be fine." He opened his car's back door for the dog, but she paced and whined. "Come on. Get in. The sooner we get this done, the sooner we can go see your mom." He attempted to scoop the husky up into the seat, but she flopped out of his hold and ducked under the door, then sat next to the passenger door. Curt slammed the back door shut. "You trying to tell me you're not a backseat driver or something?"

Bella whined and pawed the passenger door.

"Fine. But you better not shed on the upholstery." He opened the door, and Bella vaulted into the seat and made herself comfortable.

Curt chuckled and rounded the car before she decided to take over the driver's seat. Back at Annie's house, Curt let Bella off her lead into the fenced backyard, then once more retrieved his fingerprint kit from the trunk of his car.

Phil was still inspecting the furnace, accompanied by a lone firefighter named Jim.

"Hey, Phil. We'll need your prints for elimination purposes."

"No need. I always wear gloves when doing inspections." He wriggled his gloved hands.

"Perfect." Curt turned his attention to the breaker panel and managed to lift several fresh prints off the panel cover, but on the breaker that had been open, the prints were too smudged to be useful. Since Annie had been the last person to move the breaker, her print had likely smudged any others there. Next, Curt located the CO detector in the upstairs hallway and lifted five usable prints from it. He'd have to take Annie's prints to eliminate hers from the collection.

A text alert sounded on his phone. *If you're still at my place, could you bring my purple overnight bag to Grace's? It's in the bottom of my closet. Grace came to see me in the hospital and insists I stay at her house until the furnace is fixed.*

He texted back. *That's great.* He'd planned on suggesting the same thing. *Have you been released?*

Soon. Oxygen levels were already normal by the time I arrived here.

Curt sent back a thumbs-up emoticon, then went in search of Annie's overnight bag. After finding it exactly where she'd said, he returned to the basement for an update on the inspection.

Phil straightened, pushing his palms to his back to work out the kinks. "I can't find anything wrong with the furnace itself. But Jim couldn't get the snake through the exhaust pipe, so I suspect a clog of some sort. We're going to see if we can push it out from this end."

Trepidation rippled through Curt's chest. He'd been hoping Phil would find a flaw in the furnace. A blockage likely pointed to deliberate sabotage. "Keep me posted. And be sure to lock up before you leave. Ms. Bishop is going to sleep at a friend's tonight." The doors had a doorknob lock, but nothing else. He'd have to ensure Grace had dead bolts installed ASAP.

Curt retrieved Bella from the yard, and they drove to Grace's

Grace pulled into her driveway seconds after Curt arrived.

He offered Annie a hand out of the car. "Feeling better?"

"Much."

Bella let out a woof from her perch in his passenger seat and bounded across to the driver's seat and back, searching for an escape route.

"Someone's excited to see you." Curt opened his door, and Bella scampered to Annie, her entire body wiggling with delight.

Laughing, Annie gave Bella a giant hug. "Did you miss me, girl? You were a naughty girl, running after that car." She straightened with the dog's leash in hand. "Thanks for watching her."

"No problem."

Grace offered them both a cup of hot cocoa, and since Curt still had more questions for Annie, he accepted.

Annie invited him to join her in the living room, then waited until Grace disappeared into the kitchen before whispering, "Please don't mention the missing detector battery to anyone. I don't want Grace to get into trouble, or to feel that what happened is somehow her fault. She told me her handyman changes the battery, along with those in the smoke detectors, every six months. Since he has a key to the house, I'm thinking maybe he was in today for something and heard it sounding a low-battery alert, and when he couldn't find a replacement easily, he flipped the breaker until he could get back with one, but he forgot."

"That's a lot of supposition."

"But it makes sense. Anyway, his number is by the calendar hanging in the kitchen. When Grace brings the hot chocolate out, I'll go jot it down on a piece of paper and get it to you. That way you can call and ask him without having to upset Grace."

"Okay." He studied Annie, who'd clearly put a lot of thought into how to spare Grace any stress. The woman had a heart of gold. He hoped her convoluted theory was true, but the idea that Grace's handyman should happen to remove the detector's battery the same day the exhaust pipe developed a blockage was way too coincidental.

Annie gnawed on her bottom lip.

"What is it?"

"When I went downstairs to check the breaker, I caught a whiff of sandalwood."

Curt frowned. "Sandalwood?"

"It's a fragrance. The fragrance Grace's former tenant favors. I know because the bathroom cabinet smelled strongly of it when I moved in, and I still catch a whiff of it from time to time. It's probably the furnace moving stale air around. But with the breaker being off and everything, it kind of stood out to me."

"Was there anything else that stood out?"

"That's all." She pulled her feet up onto the sofa and hugged her knees.

"Here you go." Grace came into the living room carrying a tray of hot chocolate and cookies.

Curt sprang to his feet. "Let me help you with that." He relieved Grace of the tray and set it on the coffee table.

Annie scooted around her. "I'll grab napkins for us. Be right back."

Grace helped herself to a cookie and mug of hot chocolate and took a seat. "Is there a problem with the furnace? My handyman serviced it right before Annie moved in, but I suppose I need to get a dedicated furnace repairman to look at it."

"Phil's already on it."

Grace blew out a breath. "That's one worry off my mind."

Annie returned with a stack of napkins and handed the top one to Curt before taking a seat.

Curt saw a phone number in the corner of the napkin, then slid it into his pocket. "Did you have the locks changed before Annie moved in?" Curt asked Grace. If her former tenant had made a copy of his key, it would explain why Curt hadn't found evidence of a break-in that afternoon.

"No." Her gaze darted from Curt to Annie and back again. "Do you think I should?"

"It's always a good idea when changing occupants." He tried to put a positive spin on the suggestion. "You never know who might have gotten their hands on a copy of the key."

"Yes, I see what you mean. I'll ask my handyman to get right on that."

Annie squirmed, clearly unhappy at the distress he'd caused Grace.

But as far as Curt was concerned, it couldn't be helped. He couldn't chalk up two life-threatening situations in the same day to coincidence.

For some reason, Annie Bishop was being targeted.

5

*A*nnie screamed, but no sound came out. She tried to race toward her friend's crumpled car, but her legs felt as if they were pushing through waist-deep snow.

Something wet nuzzled her hand. A whine pulled her out of the nightmare.

Annie's gaze snapped to the closed blinds. She wasn't in Chicago anymore. She was safe.

For now.

Bella whined and nuzzled Annie with her wet nose once more.

Annie rolled onto her side and scratched behind Bella's ears. "I'm sorry, girl. Bad dream." She squinted at the digital clock across the room—four am. Even in her sleep, she couldn't escape Joey's reach. When she'd gone to bed, she'd tossed and turned for two hours, mentally replaying every encounter with the criminal, from the first moment he'd prevented her from strolling around a street corner into the middle of a drive-by shooting, to the night he *happened* to bump into her on a date. A date with a guy who, hours later, was killed in a hit-and-run. Shoving away the memory, she flicked on the light and sat up in bed, listening.

The rest of the house was quiet. Grace took her hearing aids out at night, so if Annie's scream had been more audible than she thought, hopefully Grace still hadn't heard it.

Bella crept onto the bed, and rather than scold her, Annie pulled her into a hug. "What are we going to do?"

Her thoughts shifted to Curt. Should she have told him about Joey? Curt's kind brown eyes had felt like a lifeline when he appeared outside the ambulance. He hadn't been on duty and she hadn't called him, but still he had come. Her heart squeezed. She scarcely knew him, yet he really seemed to care. He was certainly taking the incidents seriously, more seriously than she wanted to believe they actually were. Because if Joey was behind the attacks, the smartest thing would be to disappear again.

Her gut rebelled at the thought. She was tired of being scared. Tired of dodging people's cameras so her image wouldn't be posted online by some naive social media addict. Tired of never letting anyone get too close. Except somehow, in Safe Haven, she'd let her guard down. Grace had become a dear friend, almost a mother figure—which was not surprising, as half the people at church called her "Grandma Grace."

Annie skimmed her thumb over her fingertips. Curt had fingerprinted her to eliminate hers from the prints lifted from the house. With any luck, he'd get a hit in the police database from the others.

Annie pulled up an Internet browser on her phone and scrolled through news articles on organized crime in Chicago and then Iowa. Her heart sank at the number of hits for Iowa. It was next door to Illinois, but somehow, she hadn't imagined mobsters migrating to the Corn State.

Annie's hand strayed to Bella once more, stroking her fur. "It's not like mob bosses would make a killing strong-arming Safe Haven's mayor for the town's contracts," she muttered. "I let my imagination get the better of me." And she knew why—her client's mention of Chicago that afternoon and seeing his scar. Or more precisely, his weird reaction to her seeing it.

Annie's mind rehashed the articles she'd read and her breath stalled. Bernie said he wasn't in the military. Nor had he volunteered another noble reason for the scar, like being a police officer caught in the line of fire. What if he was connected to organized crime? What if Joey had sent Bernie to the wellness clinic to figure out if Annie Bishop and Kristie Brooks were one and the same?

I'm being paranoid.

More likely, the mechanic hadn't wanted to admit he'd missed flagging a rusted brake line when he signed off on the car's safety two months ago. And she had run over a few branches on the road. She remembered cringing at the hard thump. That could have cracked open a rusted line.

She powered off her phone. The more she thought about it, the more convinced she became. She set her phone back on the night table and nestled under the covers. "I simply had an unlucky day," she said to Bella. "Telling Curt about Joey would kick a hornet's nest full of new trouble."

As Annie walked Bella around Grace's neighborhood the next morning, she found herself scanning every shadow despite her pep talk. While the dog stopped to sniff, Annie checked her phone screen for the third time. She'd hoped to have an update on her furnace status from Curt already. Because if she could cross the carbon monoxide leak off her foul-play list, she'd have a much easier time believing Mick made a wrong call about her brake line.

By the time she returned to Grace's house, a car she didn't recognize sat in the driveway. Maybe Curt had sent someone over with news. She hurried inside.

Grace sat in the sunny kitchen sharing coffee and muffins with Bernie Dyball. At Annie's appearance, Grace sprang to her feet. "I don't think you've met my husband's friend, Bernie."

"I've missed our Saturday morning cups of coffee." Bernie acknowledged Annie with a nod, then set down his mug and fussed over Bella. "Aren't you a beautiful girl?"

Bella woofed her agreement.

Bernie laughed and snuck her a chunk of his muffin. "How long have you had a dog?"

"She's not mine. She's Annie's." Grace motioned toward Annie. "Remember I told you about Annie? She's my rental tenant, but she had to stay here last night because of trouble with her furnace." She smiled at Annie. "Bernie bowled with my late husband for years. Do you still bowl, Bernie?"

He circled his left elbow in the air. "Not since my shoulder started acting up."

"I told you that you should see Annie about that."

Annie's heart lightened. Grace, not Joey, had steered Bernie in her direction. In the words of last night's paramedic, that was one mystery solved.

"She worked wonders with my wrist," Grace went on.

"Wonders, eh?" Bernie grunted. Still hunched over the dog, Bernie squinted up at Annie, no hint of recognition in his eyes.

"He did see me. Yesterday," Annie whispered to Grace.

Grace cocked her head, a silent "oh" forming on her lips.

"Don't you remember visiting me?" Annie asked Bernie. "At Kemp's Wellness Clinic. You left a tad abruptly."

"I did?" He straightened and pulled a pair of reading glasses from his pocket as if they might help him see her better.

Her heart went out to the poor man, who clearly struggled with memory issues, perhaps an early symptom of dementia.

She'd been silly to imagine the man could've been one of Joey's spies. After all, he wouldn't have been able to remember what he was supposed to report.

Curt addressed his son in the rearview mirror as he steered onto Grace's street. "I won't be long. You need to stay in the car, okay?"

"Are you going to ask Ms. Annie to come with us?" Noah's voice rose in excitement.

Sylvie stiffened in the passenger seat.

"We'll see." Curt hadn't had the heart to cancel their annual expedition to the local orchard, but after the previous day's sabotage incidents, keeping his mind on the outing would be a challenge.

Annie must've seen him pull into the driveway, because she was outside and down the porch steps before he parked. Dark circles smudged the skin under her eyes, but a smile crinkled the corners. The smile grew even larger when she spotted Noah in the back seat and waved. "I hope the fact you have the whole family with you is good news for me."

Curt closed his car door behind him and, with a fleeting touch to the small of her back, steered her onto the porch where Noah wouldn't overhear their conversation. There was no easy way to break the worst of the news to her. "One of our officers spoke to each of your neighbors, and all of them said the car Bella chased didn't belong to anyone they knew."

Annie scanned the homes on the opposite side of Grace's street. "What about security camera footage? A camera might've picked up the car's plate number."

The hint of desperation in her tone bothered him more than it should.

When he was a rookie, an old-timer on the force had told him that when he stopped empathizing with crime victims, it was time to quit. But to survive the job, Curt had quickly learned to distance himself from their emotions as much as he could manage.

Except when it came to Annie.

"None of your neighbors have cameras," he told her. "Few people in Safe Haven do. There isn't enough crime to warrant them."

Annie deflated, and he wished he had more encouraging news for her.

"I tried locating Kai Aldred. That's Grace's former tenant, but he doesn't work Friday and Saturday nights, and his employer doesn't have a current address for him. Said Kai didn't tell him he moved. Anyway, Kai works again tomorrow evening. In the meantime, I've asked our officers to be on the lookout for him."

She wrapped her arms around her waist as if shielding herself from more bad news. "You think he messed with my brakes?"

"I won't know what to think until I talk to him. In the meantime, have you thought of anyone else who might want to settle a score with you?"

The muscle in her cheek twitched. "I guess the new round of twenty questions means the fire marshal doesn't think a furnace defect caused my CO leak."

"No defect." He cupped her shoulder reassuringly. "We will get this guy." When her eyes misted, his hand found its way to her cheek, and her breath hitched. The softness of her skin made his heart quicken. "I won't let anything happen to you." He lowered his hand. "But I need your help. I get that you aren't the kind of person who would speak ill of anyone, but think back." He withdrew his notepad and pen from his jacket pocket. "Has anything happened since you came to town that might've set someone off?"

"Trust me. I've racked my brain trying to think of anything. If you'd asked me eight years ago when I worked in the ER, I could have named some hurt and irate family members of patients we lost. But all my physical therapy clients seem happy with my services." She directed a smile at Noah.

"You worked in the ER as a physical therapist?"

Annie shrank back, glancing around them.

Curt softened his voice. "Annie?" He tilted his head until she met his gaze once more. "What are you remembering?"

She stepped back. "I was a nurse. It was very stressful. Well, being a cop, I'm sure you can imagine. Seeing people at their worst, day after day. It got to be too much. So, I changed professions."

"And that was eight years ago?"

"Yes."

He jotted the detail in his notebook. "Have any former patients from your nursing days, or their families, contacted you since you left?"

"No. None."

Grace bustled out of the house. "Curt, would you like to come in for a cup of coffee?"

"No thanks. I promised Noah I'd take him to the orchard to get apples and cider."

Grace grinned. "And do the corn maze." She turned to Annie. "It's an autumn tradition here."

"Sounds like fun." Annie's eyes clouded, and Curt didn't know what to make of her reaction.

"We'd love for you to join us." Ensuring her safety would be a lot easier if she did.

Her answering smile was noncommittal.

"Is the furnace fixed now?" Grace asked.

Curt clenched his teeth. The fire marshal had discovered the source of carbon monoxide at eleven the night before, and Curt had seen no need to ruin Annie's sleep by calling her at the time. But he'd been dreading the conversation ever since. He drew in a deep breath and held it a moment before expelling it. "There's nothing wrong with the furnace. The fire marshal found debris stuffed deep in the vent pipe, which allowed carbon monoxide to escape into the house."

"Stuffed," Annie whispered.

Curt caught her arm and steadied her when her knees suddenly gave way. Her shattered expression tore at his heart.

Grace paled. "I'm sure my handyman would've cleared the pipe when he serviced the furnace last month. And birds aren't building new nests this time of year. Was it a wasp's nest?"

Curt tightened his hold on Annie. "No, it was stones balled up in leaves."

Grace's eyes widened. "You're saying a person intentionally stuffed the pipe?"

"I'm afraid that's the way it appears."

Curt searched Annie's ashen features. But she didn't seem to see him. Her eyes were unfocused, and she remained mute.

Grace's brow furrowed. "But who would do such a horrible thing?"

6

$\mathcal{A}$nnie pressed her lips together, fighting the impulse to hyperventilate, but her breaths still came too fast. How had Joey found her? She'd been so careful.

The pressure in her chest intensified.

Perhaps it wasn't Joey at all. Could Kai be the one behind the attacks?

She drew in a long, slow breath, desperately hoping that wasn't the case. She hated to think it of anyone Grace knew, especially since Kai had autism.

At an unexpected touch to her arm, Annie jumped, then hurried to focus on Grace's conversation with Curt. "I think you should go." Grace squeezed Annie's forearm encouragingly. "It'll help take your mind off things."

"Go where?" She tracked Grace's surprised glance at Curt. "I'm sorry." She stuffed her hands in her pockets to hide their trembling. "I must've zoned out for a minute."

The concern in Curt's brown eyes almost reduced her to tears.

She fisted her hands inside her pockets, digging her nails into her palms to keep her emotions in check.

"I asked if you'd like to join Noah, Sylvie, and me on our trip to the orchard."

"Oh." She supposed an orchard was the last place Kai would expect her to be. Or Joey for that matter. She winced. If she really thought there was any chance Joey was behind what had happened to her, it was a bad idea to let herself be seen with Noah and Curt.

"It's a Safe Haven tradition, not to be missed," Curt went on, apparently taking her hesitation as a need to be convinced. "There's hot apple cider, hayrides, a corn maze, apple pies, apple fritters." He grinned. "Apple everything, really."

"Pumpkins too," Grace added. "If you bring one home, I'll make us a pie."

"It sounds lovely," Annie hedged.

"Go on," Grace urged. "Your day is wide open."

"I don't want to intrude on your family time."

"You'd be doing me a favor," Curt cajoled, the attractive dimple winking in his cheek. "If you're with me, I won't have to worry about whether you're safe."

Annie's eyes widened. She was pretty sure most police officers didn't get so personally involved with the crimes they investigated, not even in Safe Haven.

Noah lowered his window. "Did Dad ask you to come with us?"

She grinned at the boy's enthusiasm. "Yes, but I'm—"

"You've got to come," the boy insisted. "I bet you never went to any corn mazes in Alaska."

Annie chuckled. "That's true."

"You can't disappoint him." Grace nudged Annie with her elbow, the matchmaking gleam in her eye impossible to mistake.

Annie tried to ignore the twirl in her stomach. "I obviously don't want to disappoint Noah, but we don't know who's targeting me or why. I'm not sure it's a good idea to hang out where anyone could see me. It might endanger whoever's with me."

"Nonsense," Grace interjected. "You can't get much safer than spending the day with a police officer at your side."

Curt grinned. "She's got a point."

Against her better judgment, Annie lifted her hands in surrender.

"Okay, yes, I'd love to go."

Curt opened the back door so Annie could slide into the car beside Noah. Then, climbing behind the steering wheel, he ignored Sylvie's scowl. The reality was that Annie would distract him from their family time less if she was with them than worrying about her would have if she hadn't come. Besides, Noah was eager to include her in their day. Not that *Curt* was eager. He was being pragmatic. He had a responsibility to ensure Annie stayed safe until he took her attacker off the streets.

Noah chattered nonstop at Annie the entire trip to the orchard.

Curt caught her gaze in the rearview mirror. She smiled, seemingly unbothered by his son's exuberance. In fact, he thought she was enjoying it.

"Noah," Sylvie scolded. "Don't give away all the orchard's secrets before we get there. Half the fun for a newcomer is in the discovery."

Noah hung his head. "Sorry, Ms. Annie. I didn't think about that."

"No need to apologize," she assured. "I like knowing what to expect when I go someplace."

Curt doubted she'd expected to face a saboteur when she moved to Safe Haven. He signaled to pull into the farm's driveway, then parked in a back corner of the lot to leave the closer spaces for the elderly and families with young children.

Noah bounded out of the car. "Can we go on the hayride first, Dad?"

Curt eyed the open hay-laden wagon being towed by an old red tractor. "Fine, but you're sitting on an inside bale. I don't want you toppling off the back."

"But Dad, the back's the funnest place—way bumpier."

Annie laughed. "I always sat at the back of the school bus as a kid, for the same reason."

"You heard your dad," Sylvie interjected, in a tone meant to dissuade Noah from latching onto Annie's comment to appeal the edict.

Suddenly feeling like a killjoy before they'd even started, Curt peeled a ten-dollar bill out of his wallet. "I tell you what. Today, you can sit anywhere you want as long as one of us sits beside you." He handed Noah the money. "Now, go and get our tickets."

"I can pay for my own." Annie unzipped her purse.

"Don't worry about it." Curt stayed her hand, and the gentle touch sent a responding ripple through his chest. Snatching back his hand, he cleared his throat. "Save your money for Grace's pumpkin."

Annie's cheeks flushed to the exact hue of his favorite Gala apples and appeared every bit as sweet.

He groaned at the wayward thought, which betrayed an attraction he had no business feeling. He pushed it aside and focused on spotting Noah. The place wasn't big enough or busy enough to be too concerned about letting his son run ahead. And he'd rather that Annie didn't get the impression he was a helicopter dad, even if every impulse inside him made him want to be, especially with the added concern of who might have Annie in his sights.

"We might be able to catch this wagon before it leaves," Sylvie said. "If we hurry."

"We're right behind you," Curt said.

Annie fell into step behind Sylvie, and after a quick scan of their surroundings, Curt brought up the rear.

Noah intercepted them with a fistful of tickets before they reached the loading area. He gave them to the collector, then clambered onto the wagon. "Want to sit at the back with me?" he asked Annie.

Curt leaned over and caught a whiff of her vanilla scent as he whispered, "Be warned. These fields are way bumpier than any school bus ride."

"No problem. I was a roller coaster addict as a teen. I think I can handle a hayride."

Curt cocked his head. "There are roller coasters in Alaska?"

Something akin to alarm flashed in her eyes before she ducked her head. "I didn't always live in Alaska," she murmured. She joined Noah on a hay bale at the back of the wagon and surveyed the visitors milling about the grounds. "I didn't realize there'd be so many people here."

"It's a great family outing this time of year." Sylvie settled on the other side of Noah. "It tends to attract visitors from across the county."

Curt sat atop a hay bale in the middle of the wagon to face them and the trail behind, while also having a view—albeit somewhat obstructed—to the left and right of the wagon. From Annie's frequent furtive scans of her surroundings, he figured she would alert him to anyone of concern. As much as he hoped it would prove a relaxing outing for her, her vigilance in watching her surroundings was good to see.

Between apple-themed games, he was astonished at how quickly the next couple of hours sped by. With much laughter, they even competed at creating the best soap carving. Curt's attempt to carve a tree wasn't destined to win any prizes, and Noah laughed it out of the running the instant Curt held up his masterpiece for inspection. Not that Curt cared. His son's laughter was the best prize of all.

Annie watched the exchange with a hint of longing in her gaze.

"Yours is pretty good," Curt praised.

Annie frowned. "It's supposed to be a cat head."

Noah giggled. "It came out more like a frog."

Cocking her head, Annie scrutinized her creation. "You're right. I was never that great at arts and crafts."

"Aunt Sylvie is." Noah hitched his thumb toward Sylvie's carving, in the shape of a wise old grandmother.

"She's always been the creative one in the family," Curt added. "Within three years of start-up, her barefoot shoe company grew into an online business featuring footwear almost entirely of her own design."

"Yes, we often recommend them at the clinic," Annie said. "They're great."

A smile tipped the corners of Sylvie's lips as she put the finishing touches on her creation.

"Can I get a corn dog while we wait for Aunt Sylvie to finish?" Noah begged.

Annie tapped his leg. "Is that thing hollow?"

Noah's forehead scrunched, clearly not understanding the implication.

"She can't figure out where you put all the food you eat," Curt explained. "She figures you're stuffing it in a hollow leg."

Noah waved off the silly idea. "Dad says I have a high metabolism."

"Yup. I swear he burns the food off as fast as he takes it in." Curt shifted so the snack stand was within view and gave his son a five-dollar bill. "Bring your corn dog back here."

"Thanks." Noah took off so fast, he slammed into the corner of a picnic table and ricocheted into an apple crate. Grabbing his knee, he curled into a ball and wailed.

Both Sylvie and Annie sprang to his side. But Noah pulled away from Sylvie's touch.

"Take it easy," Annie soothed, coaxing him into letting her assess the damage. Crouching beside him, she carefully touched and pressed the knee in various places to evaluate its mobility, with such tenderness that Noah soon wiped away his tears. Annie then assisted him to his feet and appraised his attempts to bear weight on the injured limb.

The sight of her motherly ministrations stirred feelings in Curt he thought had died with his wife, Beth. He wasn't sure how he felt about that.

After a few tentative steps, Noah declared himself better. Then, in his typical whirlwind fashion, he gave Annie a spontaneous thank-you hug and raced off to buy his corn dog.

"I'll go with him," Sylvie volunteered, gathering up their soap carvings before giving chase.

"Apparently you have the magic touch," Curt said with more than a hint of admiration in his voice.

The adorable red hue flushed her cheeks once more. "I have a lot of experience with cranky knees."

With a soft touch to the small of her back, Curt steered her in the direction Noah and Sylvie had taken, even as he reminded himself that he'd invited Annie to join them so he could keep a protective eye on her. That was all.

By the time they caught up to Noah and Sylvie, Noah had already inhaled half his corn dog.

"Okay." Curt clapped his hands together to secure Noah's full attention. "Time for the corn maze. And then we'll help Annie pick a pumpkin for Grandma Grace before heading home. Got it?" He'd learned years ago to prepare Noah for their pending departure, because there always seemed to be one more activity he simply *had* to do before they left.

Noah visibly deflated at Curt's words. But he didn't argue. Trying to impress Annie, perhaps? He confirmed Curt's suspicion when he caught Annie's hand. "C'mon, let's race Dad and Aunt Sylvie through the maze."

The pair took off, leaving Sylvie looking dejected.

"You feeling like chopped liver too?" Curt nudged his sister with his elbow. "C'mon, let's show them how this maze is done."

Curt and Sylvie raced after Annie and Noah, but three turns later, still hadn't found them. Curt retraced his steps to the previous turn and detoured along the second option. A hum of voices and laughter drifted through the tall corn walls on either side.

Then a bloodcurdling scream silenced the babble—Annie's scream.

A hand shot through the corn wall and clamped onto Annie's arm. The scream tore out of her before she fully understood what was happening.

"Noah, run." Annie twisted away in an attempt to break the grip.

Instead of running, Noah bit her attacker's wrist.

The guy yelped, and Annie jerked free, grabbing Noah's hand to race back to Curt.

"What did you do that for?" the guy bellowed, plowing through the corn wall.

Recognizing his voice, Annie spun around. "Colin Mitchell." She planted her hands on her hips. "What do you think you're playing at?"

Two more teens scrabbled through the corn wall, doubling over with laughter. "He told us he could scare you good. But you showed him."

"She didn't scare me," Colin countered. "She bit me."

"That was me." Noah beamed with pride.

"Let me see the bite mark." Annie reached for the teen's arm.

Curt rounded the corner and charged toward Colin. In a flash, he grabbed Colin by the shoulders and pinned the kid with a menacing stare.

"Curt, stop," Annie said as the other two boys scrambled back through the corn wall. "He's one of my clients, playing a prank."

Struggling to catch her breath, Sylvie caught Noah in a bear hug and drew him away from the ruckus.

"Terrorizing defenseless women and children isn't a prank, it's a crime," Curt ranted, letting go of Colin.

As much as Colin had frightened her, Annie felt sorry for the teen, who'd clearly meant no real harm. "It's fine, really. It was all in good-natured fun."

Colin cast Annie a small but grateful smile. "I'm really sorry I scared you, Ms. Bishop."

"Isn't that exactly what you wanted to do?" Curt growled.

Colin ducked his head. "Yes, sir. I just didn't think she would—"

"That's right," Curt interjected. "You didn't think. Don't let me catch you pulling a stunt like that again."

"Yes sir. I mean no sir." Colin's red face darkened three more shades. "I mean, I won't. I promise."

Curt glared at the young man. "Go. Now."

Colin didn't need to be told twice. He took off at a sprint, wiped out in the mud at the first corner, and had to scramble to regain his footing before disappearing down the next leg of the maze.

Curt's hands fisted at his sides. "Let's go home."

"We still have to pick out a pumpkin for Grandma Grace," Noah reminded him.

"Right. Let's do that." Curt motioned Noah and Sylvie onward through the maze and seemed determined to avoid eye contact with Annie.

Was he mad at her for causing his overreaction? She fell into step beside him. "I'm sorry I screamed."

"You have nothing to be sorry for." He reminded her of a tightly wound coil. Even his voice radiated tension. "Are you hurt?"

"No, but I'm a little shaken. I didn't see Colin at first, because he stuck his arm through the corn wall. And I've been on edge since yesterday."

"Understandable."

"Noah was amazing. I told him to run, but he jumped to my rescue and bit Colin's arm."

Curt squared his jaw.

Bothered by Curt's clear disapproval of his son's involvement, Annie added, "He was very brave." Sure, Noah hadn't done as he was told, but his heart had been in the right place.

"Yes, but we might not have said the same if our prankster had been your saboteur."

Sylvie shot a silencing scowl over her shoulder at Curt. "Why don't you help Noah pick a pumpkin for Grandma Grace?" she urged, exchanging places with Curt. "Go on."

Acting somewhat cheerier, Curt headed with Noah toward the pumpkin patch.

"Please forgive my brother's moodiness," Sylvie said. "I'm afraid those teens triggered disturbing memories."

"Oh?"

Sylvie clasped Annie's arm, drawing her to a stop, then glanced at Curt and Noah and waited until they moved out of earshot before continuing. "Curt's wife was killed by a trio of teens who invaded their house."

Annie gasped. She pictured Curt's fisted hands and tense stance after she'd convinced him to release Colin. No wonder he'd struggled to calm down after the incident. "I had no idea."

"It's not something Curt likes to talk about. And it's probably better if you don't tell him you heard the story from me."

"Of course." Annie's heart ached for the man. How she wished her reaction to Colin's prank hadn't resurrected such painful memories.

"So, what's your story?" Sylvie asked.

"My story?"

"Your scream. You sounded terrified. I figure there has to be a reason."

Annie slowed her pace, suddenly overwhelmed by the weight of the secret she'd carried alone for the past eight years. "I'm not sure what you mean. Colin startled me—that's all."

Sylvie's raised eyebrow intimated that she was unconvinced. "Your reaction reminded me of my college roommate after her ex started stalking her."

Annie's heart stuttered, and in that instant, she was back in Chicago, her frustration with the guy who "happened" to run into her too many times a week, escalating into fears that he'd started painting bull's-eyes on the backs of any guy she so much as talked to.

"Oh, yeah," Sylvie said. "I know that expression."

Annie blew out a breath. "A long time ago, before I moved to Alaska, a guy did stalk me." She bit her lip, as stunned by her admission as Sylvie. "Please don't tell Curt," she pleaded. Not that she suspected for one second that Curt might be corrupt. But what if he talked to other officers? Word could get back to Joey.

Sylvie's head tilted, and Annie winced. Of course Sylvie would think the request odd. Of all the people to confide in, why had she chosen a cop's sister?

"Curt mentioned that someone sabotaged your house," Sylvie probed. "Don't you think he needs to know your stalker might have found you again?"

"No." Annie gulped. "I mean, he hasn't found me. There's no way. I changed my name, my profession, and my state. Joey Carmello is the least of my worries." She clamped her mouth shut. What was she doing? She hadn't so much as breathed the name of the mob boss's son in eight years. "Please forget I said anything."

Sylvie drew her into a warm hug. "It's okay. I understand."

Tears pressed at Annie's eyes as a weight lifted from her shoulders. *Lord, don't let this have been a mistake.*

By the time Curt and Noah presented Annie with their chosen pumpkin, Curt had regained a grip on his emotions. He'd have to thank his sister later for the save. She'd obviously realized he needed a chance to cool off after the run-in with the kid. It wasn't as if he hadn't had to deal with delinquent teens since his wife's death, but Annie's terrified scream had churned up too many memories. And the fact that Noah had been with her at the time had catapulted his fears to the stratosphere.

If Annie hadn't come to that clueless teen's defense— Curt cut off the thought. He didn't want to think what he might have done.

Annie passed a tray of steaming cups of hot apple cider to Curt. "I figured we could enjoy one last treat before we leave," she said with a wink, then lifted the winning pumpkin from Noah's hold and admired their selection.

"I picked a big one at first," Noah confessed, "but Dad says the smaller ones are better for pies."

"I'm glad he knew that," she said, her smile sweeter than the cider. "I might've picked a big one myself."

They sipped their cider as they ambled toward the parking lot. "Do you need to pick up anything from your house before I take you back to Grace's?" Curt asked.

"Actually, Mick texted to let me know my car is ready. Could you drop me off there instead?"

"Sure, but you're going to stay at Grace's another night yet, right?"

A shadow eclipsed her cheery disposition. "Do you think that's necessary?"

"I think it's wise. While I'm sure Bella would alert you to an intruder, until we locate Kai and Grace gets your locks changed, we can't be sure who else has a key to the place."

Annie shivered. "I need to stop by my place for more clothes." She plucked at her hoodie. "I prefer to dress in something a little nicer for church."

Noah had mentioned that his physical therapist attended their church, but between one thing and another, Curt had never gotten around to introducing himself. An unfortunate oversight on his part. He would've liked to have become acquainted under happier circumstances.

"Is that a problem?" Annie's question jolted Curt from his thoughts.

"No. No problem. I'll take you there before I drop you at Mick's. That way you won't have to go to the house alone."

She sucked in a breath as if she might protest, but apparently changed her mind with a glance at Noah. "I appreciate that."

Oddly, Sylvie didn't seem to appreciate the detours. She remained almost sullenly mute the entire ride home. She waved goodbye to Annie and even managed a smile when they delivered her to Mick's Garage, but then her attention immediately returned to the front windshield, her hands clutched tightly in her lap.

Curt walked Annie to her car. "I guess we'll see you in church tomorrow morning. But you have my number. Don't hesitate to call if anything concerning happens."

Annie clasped his arm, her touch sending a warm rush straight to the center of his chest. "Thank you for including me in your family outing."

"We enjoyed having you," he said honestly, then waited until she'd climbed into her car and driven away before rejoining Noah and Sylvie.

"It was fun having Ms. Annie with us today," Noah said. "Don't you think?"

"Yes, she's very nice."

Sylvie crossed her arms over her chest, her gaze still fixed on the windshield.

Curt elbowed his sister. "In case you think I didn't notice, I appreciate you bailing me out back in the corn maze earlier by spending time with Annie."

Sylvie pressed her lips together so tightly that the color seeped from them.

Okay, what is going on there? He decided to wait until they were home and Noah had found something to occupy his attention, before getting to the bottom of Sylvie's suddenly foul mood. He'd thought she liked Annie.

An hour later, as Curt heated the barbecue for their supper, Sylvie tromped outside with a plate of burgers, letting the screen door slap noisily behind her.

"Out with it," Curt ordered. "What has you so steamed?"

"For someone so paranoid about keeping your son safe, don't you think you're being a little reckless?"

"Because I invited Annie to join us today?"

"Yes." She frowned back at the house, where Noah was doing his math homework, and lowered her voice to a hiss. "You're obviously worried this guy will come after her again, so how could you even think of endangering Noah by letting her anywhere near him?"

He bristled at the accusation. "The guy isn't going to come after her in broad daylight in a place full of people with a cop at her side."

"From where I was standing, it sure didn't look like that's what you thought when you tackled that teen."

Curt grimaced. "Admittedly not my finest hour. Her scream made me panic."

"And rightly so. I think you should remember that feeling the next time you're tempted to include her in a family outing so you can play bodyguard."

Noah stomped his foot, having emerged from the house without either of them noticing. "I like Ms. Annie. And if she needs help, I think we should help her. Isn't that the right thing to do, Dad?"

"Yes, but your aunt is right too. How we help shouldn't put you in danger."

"But—"

"We can discuss this later. Right now, you need to finish your homework while Aunt Sylvie and I finish our discussion."

Noah spun on his heel and stormed back inside.

"I don't want to be the bad guy here," Sylvie said. "But there's more going on than Annie's let you in on."

The accusation hit him like a sucker punch. "How so?"

Sylvie bit her lip. "I don't want to betray her confidence."

Curt leveled a frown at his sister. "It's a bit late for that, don't you think?"

She gave up. "The way she reacted to the corn maze prank reminded me how paranoid Karen used to be."

Curt flinched. Her roommate had been plagued by a stalker for two semesters before suddenly disappearing. If Sylvie was reliving the dark times, no wonder she'd been acting strangely.

"I mentioned Karen's experience to Annie," Sylvie went on, "to see how she'd react."

"And?"

"She admitted to having a stalker. Someone named Joey Carmello."

Curt's heart stuttered. "She said that?" *And didn't tell me?*

"Yeah, but she didn't mean to and immediately begged me not to share it with you."

Curt felt gutted. He thought Annie trusted him.

"She insisted Joey couldn't be behind the attacks," Sylvie explained.

"How could she be so sure?"

"She said they happened before she moved to Alaska."

He recalled the alarm that had flashed in her eyes when he questioned the existence of roller coasters in Alaska. "She mentioned she hadn't always lived in Alaska."

"She hasn't always been Annie Bishop either. That's why she's convinced herself Joey couldn't have found her. She hasn't heard from him since she changed her name, her profession, and her state."

If Annie had gone to such lengths to get away from the guy, he must have been terrible. No wonder she didn't want to believe the sabotage could be his work.

"So"—Sylvie slapped a burger onto the grill, as if to punctuate the word—"now you understand why I don't want her anywhere near our family."

Curt narrowed his eyes. "No, I don't. After what happened to your roommate, you of all people should know we can't abandon Annie. She needs friends to watch out for her more than ever."

"You seem to be blurring some lines here. You're a cop. Not her friend."

Curt winced. "I can be both."

Sylvie raised an eyebrow. "Like I said, I don't want to be the bad guy here. I'm just trying to keep Noah safe."

"You know Noah's safety is my top priority." It had been his whole reason for going to Annie's office in the first place. He hated to think what might've happened to Annie yesterday if he hadn't spotted the puddle of brake fluid under her car.

"In your head, yes. Make sure your actions align with it." She zipped up her sweater jacket. "I won't stay for supper. I need to be off." She started across the yard toward her house next door.

"Come on, you don't have to leave. You know I appreciate that you always have Noah's best interests at heart."

Sylvie didn't even slow down. "I'll see you tomorrow." She disappeared into her house.

That evening, Curt had a long conversation with Noah about how to respond to strangers, while trying not to terrify him.

"I know we need to be careful, Dad," his son finally said in exasperation. "But it's not right to stay away from Ms. Annie. You've always told me we're supposed to do for others what we'd want them to do for us."

Curt stifled a smirk at having his lecture used against him. "That's true. But you are a young boy, and Ms. Bishop—"

"David was a boy when he killed Goliath," Noah interjected.

"You're right. He was." Curt swallowed a groan. "But David's people were at war. You won't be killing anyone, understood?"

With a duck of his head, Noah conceded that much, and Curt tucked his son into bed. He'd never thought his son's bedtime Bible stories would be used against him. The boy would make a great lawyer someday. And the truth was, as concerned as Curt was for Noah's safety, he was proud of his son's courage too.

Curt wished he'd thought through the risks of including Annie in today's activities before inviting her. Because what if Annie was wrong about Joey Carmello, and the stalker had found her?

And what if he'd seen her with Noah?

Sunday morning, Curt lingered outside the church doors. Neither Grace's nor Annie's car was in the parking lot, and it wasn't like Grace to arrive at the last minute. He scanned the perimeter of the property but didn't spot anyone lurking about. If they hadn't been running late themselves, he would've driven past Grace's house to ensure Annie's saboteur hadn't located her there. Grinding his teeth, he debated whether he should do that anyway.

When he'd attempted to run a background check on Joey Carmello the night before, he didn't like what he learned. He'd found a handful of Carmellos in the system, most of them from the Chicago area, three of them Josephs. One of them was under fifty. If Annie's former stalker was one of those Carmellos, he was involved in organized crime—the kind of guy who always got what he wanted. Or someone would pay.

Curt checked the time on his cell phone and made sure he hadn't missed a call or text.

Sylvie poked her head out the front doors of the church. "If you're out here watching for Annie, she's already inside. Gayle and Ian gave her and Grace a ride."

Curt's breath escaped in an embarrassingly audible *whoosh*. "Thanks." Catching a ride had been a smart precaution. One he wished he'd thought of for her.

Sylvie winked, apparently having forgiven him for yesterday.

They sat three rows behind Annie and Grace, which suited Curt. He didn't expect trouble inside the church building, but from where he sat, he could watch for it. He'd feel a lot better once they found Grace's former tenant and compared his prints to those lifted from the brake line and furnace pipe. Kai was scheduled to work that night, which left less than twelve hours to ensure he didn't find Annie again before they found him, assuming he was their culprit.

If he wasn't, Curt would have to ask Annie about Carmello. But he hoped she'd trust him with the information of her own volition before it came to that.

Sylvie elbowed him to take the offering plate the usher held.

Jerking his attention back to the service, Curt added his donation and passed the plate on to his sister.

At the end of the service, she elbowed him again. "Good sermon, Pastor Alan gave, eh?"

Curt nodded automatically. "Yes, good food for thought."

Sylvie rolled her eyes. "For a cop, you're not all that observant. Pastor Tim spoke today."

Curt blinked. "Really?"

Sylvie chuckled. "I'm kidding."

"Cute," he said dryly.

He caught up to Annie outside as she gave a fatherly-looking man an exuberant hug. Fearful the affectionate display might set off her stalker, Curt surreptitiously glanced about the parking lot and perimeter.

"Curt." Annie motioned him closer, her soft blue eyes and smile drawing him more than they should. "This is Ray Adams, Grace's handyman. He's offered to install security sensors and an alarm at the house, in addition to new locks." She beamed, as if sincerely confident the measures would keep danger at bay.

He admired her resilience, but unfortunately, he knew better. Not that extra security wasn't a good start. Curt shook the man's hand. "A camera would be a welcome addition too," Curt suggested. "Speaking as a police officer, there's nothing like a good visual to garner the public's assistance in catching a suspect."

Grace agreed. "Whatever the cost, Ray."

"You've got it. I should be able to pick up everything I need tomorrow morning and have the installation done by day's end."

After Annie thanked Ray again, Curt asked about her afternoon plans.

Her warm smile banished his dark thoughts. "I'm hiking at Pikes Peak State Park with Ian and Gayle."

"Nice. I haven't been there in years. Mind if I tag along?"

Sylvie glared at him.

Annie's smile faltered. "It's probably better if you don't. Noah's well-being should be your first concern."

Unable to argue with that, Curt clenched his jaw.

"Don't worry about me." Annie motioned to her friends. "Ian has military training. He won't let anything happen to us."

"Good to hear." Curt touched her hand. "But don't hesitate to call if you have any concerns." He resisted adding a list of other things to be worried about. Since she'd dealt with a stalker in the past, he suspected she was well acquainted with hypervigilance.

Sylvie was heading to an out-of-town craft show for the afternoon, so Curt treated Noah to hot dogs and fries from his favorite fast-food restaurant, and then they grabbed Noah's soccer ball from home and headed to the park to kick it around.

Several of Noah's friends soon joined them. "How about you be the goalie?" Noah's friend Jamie asked Curt. "And we can all take shots on you."

At the chorus of agreement that followed, Curt obliged. Several dozen shots later, Jamie's mother rescued him with the announcement of fresh-baked cookies for all.

Afterward, as they walked home from the park, clouds piled up in the sky, blotting out the sun, much like Noah's sudden mood shift. "I wish I had a mom."

"You have Aunt Sylvie," Curt reminded him.

Noah kicked a stone from the sidewalk. "It's not the same."

Curt squeezed his son's shoulder, pretty sure Noah wasn't referring to Sylvie's low-carb baking kick. "You're right. It's not the same." Yes, his sister helped with all the motherly tasks, but Curt still missed having a partner to come home to, to share his life with. His thoughts drifted to Annie, as they'd done often throughout the afternoon. He and his wife used to love to hike. They'd bundled Noah in the backpack-style baby carrier and gone out for hours.

When they reached the house, another of Noah's friends ran over from his yard. "Hey, can I play here for a while? My baby brother is napping, and Mom said I have to be quiet."

Noah shot an eager glance at Curt. "Is that okay, Dad?"

"Of course." Curt unlocked the front door. "Come on in, Shane."

With Noah and his friend occupied in the family room, Curt took advantage of the opportunity to reach out to the Chicago PD. Annie might not want to believe her former stalker was behind the sabotage, but Curt would rather operate on facts.

A desk sergeant answered the nonemergency line.

"I'm with Safe Haven PD in Iowa," Curt said by way of introduction. "I'm looking for information on a member of an organized crime family working out of Chicago, the Carmellos. Can you connect me with someone who could help with that?"

"Please hold," the sergeant said, without asking for details or offering any sense of whether someone was in who would have the information.

Calling on a Sunday was a long shot. As the minutes wore on, second thoughts crept through Curt's mind. Mob informants within the police department might leak his request to the wrong people. He shouldn't have mentioned where he was calling from. The call had been a calculated risk. Because if Joey didn't know where Annie was, learning an officer from a small town in Iowa was asking about him might make him curious enough to ask more questions. Maybe even come searching for her again.

Curt abruptly ended the call before the sergeant came back on the line. There must be a safer way to get the information he was after. Pacing his office, he thought of his buddy with Orlando PD, and decided to give him a call.

"Sure, I don't mind making the inquiry for you," his friend said. "If we get word he's hopped a plane to Florida after that, we'll know the department has a leak."

"And at least I'll know Carmello is heading for the other side of the country." And that the probability he was behind the attacks on Annie was slim. "I appreciate you doing this for me."

"Hey, no problem. But it might be better if I wait until tomorrow morning. I'm more likely to reach a detective in the organized crime squad."

"Sounds good." They spent a few more minutes catching up on each other's lives before ending the call. Curt had to hope his call to Chicago PD hadn't been recorded.

Annie drew in Bella's leash to stop her from racing after every sound and smell and tangling herself around the trees. She didn't dare let the husky loose for fear she'd run after something and get lost. After that had happened twice in Alaska, Annie decided never to risk it again. Drawn by the panoramic view, Annie paused at the edge of a cliff and inhaled the pine-scented air.

But the tranquil scene couldn't vanquish the fears plaguing her thoughts. Guilt gnawed at her for not telling Curt about Joey and for swearing Sylvie to secrecy.

Annie couldn't blame the woman for the scowl she'd given her brother when he practically invited himself to join them on the hike. Annie expelled a sigh. Maybe telling Sylvie about Joey was a good thing, however remote the possibility that he was behind the attacks. At least Sylvie would be sure to safeguard Noah.

Admittedly, Annie had been a little surprised that Curt—the man who'd been hesitant to let his son return to soccer practice after an injury—hadn't balked at the idea of allowing her anywhere near Noah when she clearly had a target on her back.

Gayle stood beside her and scratched Bella. "You're still thinking about the sabotage?"

"That obvious?"

"You've been pretty quiet. Not that I blame you. I'd be totally freaked out if that stuff happened to me. And don't hate me, but as much as I want Officer Porter to figure out who's behind the attacks, I really hope it's not Mom's former tenant. She'd be devastated. I'm so grateful you convinced the cops not to mention anything about their suspicions to her until they know for sure."

"I saw no point in worrying her." They picked their way down the steep trail, following Ian's lead.

Halfway down, Gayle said, "Do you have any idea who else your saboteur could be?"

Annie shook her head, not trusting her voice.

"I'm sorry. I'll stop talking about it. Hikes are supposed to take our minds off our troubles."

Annie stopped and turned to face Gayle. "Actually, I've been trying to find a way to tell you. I'm considering leaving the practice and Safe Haven altogether." She added the last part in a whisper.

"What? No. You can't let this guy drive you away. This place could be so good for you."

Bella whined as if voicing her agreement.

Annie tightened her grip on the dog's leash. "But what if he comes after me again? At the clinic next time? I can't put the safety of our clients at risk."

Ian hiked back to where the pair had stopped. "Don't you worry about the clinic," he declared in a deep bass voice that would make any criminal cower.

"Yeah," Gayle seconded. "Like you told the officer, Ian is ex-military and more than capable of providing all the security we need at the clinic." She beamed at her husband, who winked his thanks for her vote of confidence.

A whisper of longing tugged at Annie's heart at the loving exchange.

"Besides," Gayle added, "it's times like this when you need your friends around."

"That's true," Ian agreed. "I always counted on my team to have my back in battle. And with the cops watching out for you outside of work, and us watching your back at the clinic, you're safer here than anywhere."

Annie squirmed. She appreciated their encouragement but was certain they wouldn't feel as brave if she admitted a mobster's son could be behind the attacks—the kind of guy who got what he wanted, no matter the cost.

Gayle prodded them onward. "After all, what's to stop the guy from following you wherever you move? You're better off here, where you have friends to watch out for you."

The sound of stone hitting stone cracked above their heads.

"Get down." Ian tackled them, sheltering their bodies with his own.

Something missed Annie's shoulder by a hair's breadth. Then Bella yelped as it bounced off her back. "Someone's throwing stones over the cliff edge."

Ian shuffled them toward the shelter of an overhang, grunting as a stone caught him. Gayle cried out in pain.

"Hey, stop throwing stones," Ian bellowed, his deep voice booming off the rock face. "There are people down here."

Another rock sailed over the edge and Annie curled into a ball over Bella, shielding them both with her arms. "He's aiming at us."

9

"Officer Porter?" verified the male voice on the other end of the phone.

"Yes, who's this?" Curt left the family room to take the call in private.

"Clayton County Sheriff's Department. We received an emergency call from Pikes Peak, and the caller asked that we also notify you of the attack."

Curt's heart rammed into his throat. "Annie Bishop? Is she okay?" He raced to his bedroom to grab his gun and holster. He knew he should have gone hiking with her.

"The caller was Ian Kemp. No word yet on the condition of the victims. Fire, medical, and deputies have been dispatched to the scene."

"I'm the investigating officer in two recent attacks on Ms. Bishop, who was hiking with the Kemps." Curt strode to the family room and whispered to Noah to put on his coat and ask his friend to head home.

"That must be why the caller asked that you be notified. But this is outside your jurisdiction."

"I'm still coming. ETA twenty-five minutes." He hustled Noah into the car, then careened out of the driveway.

"What's going on?" Noah asked. "Is Aunt Sylvie hurt?"

"No. We're going to see Ms. Annie at Pikes Peak." He told his phone to call Sylvie.

"Curt? What's wrong?" Sylvie's voice came over the car's hands-free system.

"Can you meet us at Pikes Peak? Something's happened to Annie."

Hearing the panic in his voice, he stole a glance at Noah and drew a long, deep breath to tamp down his rampaging fears. He'd known the woman less than forty-eight hours. Where was his reaction coming from?

"Did you hear me?" Sylvie shouted. "Where's Noah?"

Curt blocked out his mental and emotional roller coaster and focused on the road in front of him. "With me. That's why I need you to meet us there."

"But Pikes Peak isn't your jurisdiction."

"This is my case, and we're already on our way." Curt clenched his jaw against the full-blown panic threatening to erupt. "Now, can you meet us there to watch Noah or not?"

"I can. But you'd better pray Annie's stalker doesn't conclude that you have a personal interest in her."

"You're on speaker, Sylvie," Curt growled.

"See you there." The connection went dead.

"Is Ms. Annie hurt?" Noah's voice wobbled.

"I don't know," Curt answered honestly.

"What's a stalker?"

Curt cringed, wishing he'd called Sylvie privately before loading Noah into the car. "A stalker is someone who harasses another person or gives them too much unwanted attention."

"Like Lucy from my class always asking me to go to the pool with her last summer? And when I wouldn't, she told lies about me."

"Kind of like that." Curt blew out a breath, unaware of how strong the little girl's preoccupation with Noah had gotten.

"We should get Aunt Sylvie to talk to him. After she talked to Lucy's mom and dad, Lucy left me alone."

Curt wished it were that simple. "We're not sure who's harassing Ms. Bishop. That's why I haven't been able to stop him. But hopefully, today's incident will change that."

Noah clasped his hands and squeezed his eyes closed. "I'll pray you can catch him."

Curt admired his son's faith and echoed Noah's prayer, adding his own silent prayer for his son's safety, all the while second-guessing his decision to bring him along in the first place. At Noah's amen, Curt phoned the station.

Officer Jones answered on the first ring.

"Any hits yet on the fingerprints collected in the Bishop case?" Curt asked.

"After eliminating those belonging to Bishop, her handyman, and the mechanic, we zeroed in on a thumbprint and a fingerprint found on the furnace exhaust pipe and a different print found on her car's brake line. We're still running those through the system, as well as a second distinct thumbprint lifted from the CO detector."

So, someone was in the house. Curt tightened his grip on the steering wheel. "Thanks. Keep me posted. I'm responding to a call at Pikes Peak involving Ms. Bishop. Could be the same perp."

"Will do," Jones responded with a welcome note of urgency in his tone. Not that the man could speed up the computer search.

Curt swerved into the parking lot at Pikes Peak, already populated with a fire engine, an ambulance, and two sheriff's deputy vehicles. He scanned the other vehicles and spotted Sylvie sitting in her car at the far end of the lot. He parked next to her and ushered Noah to his aunt's car as she stepped out. "Thanks for coming."

She responded with a cool glare.

Understanding that her anger stemmed from concern for Noah's welfare, Curt didn't take it personally. In fact, he kind of appreciated it. He hunkered down on one knee and gave Noah a hug. "You stay with Aunt Sylvie. Do what she says. I'll be home soon."

Noah pouted. "Can't we stay? I want to see Ms. Annie."

"You can't right now, but I'll see if we can arrange a visit later."

Noah relented, but his frown left no doubt how he felt about the situation.

Curt faced the emergency vehicles as a firefighter escorted Annie to the waiting ambulance. Relief shot through Curt with such intensity that his feet took off at a sprint before his mind registered the impulse.

Annie's heart leaped at the sight of Curt racing toward her.

Concern etched deep lines in his face. "Are you hurt?"

"Just a few bruises from scrambling for cover. Ian got a nasty one from a rock that hit his back."

"He's lucky it missed his head," interjected the young female paramedic wrapping Gayle's sprained ankle.

"Someone threw rocks at you?" Curt's usual baritone voice rose to a pitch Annie hadn't heard before.

"Little ones." Ian wrangled in Bella, who'd wanted to join the deputies in their hunt for the culprits.

"Did you get hit?" Curt asked Annie.

"No," she said, but he studied her carefully for a moment, as if trying to make sure she was okay.

Once he seemed satisfied she hadn't been injured, the lines creasing his brow disappeared, giving him a sunnier appearance—one any woman would consider attractive. But she had no right to notice. She'd given up that right when Joey's equally intense concern for her welfare had escalated into much worse.

She shivered at the unbidden memories.

Curt shrugged out of his jacket and dropped it over her shoulders.

"The sheriff's deputies figure our stone throwers were kids who didn't realize the danger," Ian said. "Apparently, the park had a similar incident in the spring. And they found fresh mountain bike tracks on the trail higher up the hill to where we were walking, same as last time."

"Kids? Are you sure?" Curt's gaze returned to Annie's, simmering with uncertainty and a spark of hope.

"I was too busy diving for cover to see who was doing the throwing," she told him.

"But they stopped after I shouted at them," Ian added. "Something I figured her attacker wouldn't be inclined to do."

"You said *they*. There was more than one person?" Curt asked.

Ian lifted his ball cap and plowed his hand through his hair. "I can't say for sure. The deputy said there were three separate bike tracks."

"The deputies are scouting the trails for the culprits now," Gayle added.

"Were you hit?" Curt asked Gayle, gesturing to her ankle.

"I sprained my ankle scrambling for cover."

A deputy joined them. "Our suspects appear to be long gone."

"But you're fairly certain they were kids?" Curt spit the word with scarcely contained fury and narrowed his eyes. "Ian said you've had incidents like this before."

The deputy stiffened. "Yeah. You know how kids are. They love to watch the rocks bounce and don't realize they could hurt someone walking the paths below."

"They should realize." Curt's hands fisted. "There ought to be warning signs posted."

Remembering what Sylvie told her about kids attacking Curt's wife, Annie touched his arm. "It's all right."

He jerked away from her touch. "No, it's not. You don't understand what it's like to lose someone you love to the actions of a senseless kid."

He scrubbed his hand over his face. "I can't go through that again."

Annie's heart pinched. Was he saying he cared for her?

"No one is losing anyone," Gayle interjected.

"Right," Ian agreed.

Curt responded with a tight smile, his reddened cheeks betraying his embarrassment at the outburst.

Noah dashed up and wrapped his arms around Annie's waist. "I'm glad you're okay."

Her heart swelled as she hugged him back.

Sylvie apologized to Curt and attempted to pry Noah away. "Come on, Noah, we need to go."

"No." Noah clung tighter to Annie. "I want to stay with Dad and Ms. Annie."

"You're so sweet," Annie murmured. She shot Curt a helpless glance.

Curt squeezed his son's shoulder. "You don't talk to your aunt that way. Ms. Annie still needs to give her statement to the deputies, so you need to head home with Aunt Sylvie. I promise we won't be long."

Noah hesitated a moment but then begrudgingly complied with his father's instruction.

Once Noah was out of earshot, the deputy said, "I think we already have all the information we can glean about the culprits."

"Did Ms. Bishop tell you she was the victim of two prior attacks that could be connected?" Curt asked.

"You think the same culprit is behind this?" the deputy asked her.

Annie gulped. "I don't know."

"We shouldn't rule it out," Curt added.

"Unfortunately, there's not much more we can do. My crew are questioning hikers and taking names," the deputy said to Curt.

"Did you dust the rocks for fingerprints?" Curt asked.

"Seriously?" Annie said. "That's possible?"

"It's challenging but doable," the deputy said. "But in this case, I'm not sure how we could figure out which rocks were thrown versus which were already on the ground."

"I can walk back and help with that," Ian volunteered. He squeezed Gayle's hand. "Will you be all right here for a few minutes?"

The paramedic placed an ice pack on Gayle's freshly wrapped ankle. "Don't be long. She should have the ankle x-rayed to rule out a fracture."

Ian kissed Gayle's cheek and returned Bella's leash to Annie. "I'll be as quick as I can."

"Take all the time you need," Gayle replied. "If this attack is connected to the others, we need to get to the bottom of it."

Annie's heart squeezed with appreciation for her friend's support, especially given the pain her sprain had to be causing.

Curt read something on his phone. "We've got a lead. A fingerprint lifted from your brake line matches one left behind by an armed robber who held up a Chicago bank ten years ago."

"A bank robber?" Gayle scrunched her face. "Why would he be after Annie?"

Annie felt as if her world was imploding. Had she treated the bank robber in the ER in Chicago? Was it time to come clean about her former life? Or time to run again?

"Hard to say," Curt responded to Gayle's question. "The crook was never caught, so we don't know *who* he is. Presuming he'd been in his early twenties to midforties at the time, he could now be in his early thirties to midfifties."

"That's quite an age range." Annie failed to keep the quaver from her voice. Did mob guys like Joey rob banks or simply shake down mom-and-pop shops for "protection" money?

"The prints lifted from your furnace pipe and CO monitor are different," Curt added, "but that doesn't rule out my suspicion the same guy was behind both. As soon as I pick up Kai from his job tonight and print him, we'll be able to confirm whether he's our man."

"I've met Kai," Gayle said. "I'm not sure if he's lived here all his life and I don't know his age for sure, but I'd be surprised if he's any older than his late twenties, which would have made him a teen when that robbery occurred."

"Plenty of teens commit armed robbery," Curt acknowledged grimly, his darkened expression suggesting he was remembering his wife's deadly encounter.

But as much as Annie hated to wish it of Grace's former tenant, proving Kai was their culprit would be a relief. Because otherwise, chances were the bank robbery was the work of one of Joey's minions—if not Joey himself.

10

The sun skulked behind the clouds as Curt glanced in the rearview and side mirrors for the umpteenth time. Annie sat in the passenger seat with Bella in the back. He suspected that the reason Annie allowed him to drive her home to Safe Haven instead of accompanying her friends to the hospital was because she thought they'd be safer without her around.

Ian had pulled Curt aside and confided that, before the rock-throwing incident, Annie told Gayle she was thinking about leaving town for the same reason. His thoughts had been doing somersaults ever since, trying to come up with a way to change her mind.

The sight of Annie outside the ambulance had swallowed him whole and spit him out. Add to that the guilt gnawing at him for Sylvie's gutted expression when Noah declared he wanted to stay with Annie instead of going home with his aunt. Curt would have to make that up to his sister somehow.

But first he had to figure out how to convince Annie she'd be safer staying in Safe Haven than running.

"I'm sorry you've had such a rough few days," he told her.

Annie stared out the side window, hair hiding her face. But her hunched shoulders suggested that *rough* didn't begin to describe how she felt.

When she didn't respond, he tried again. "If the deputy is right about the rock throwers being kids, the fingerprint match from the brake line might be good news."

Her gaze snapped to his, her forehead creased in confusion. "How?"

Her bewilderment seemed genuine, so maybe she honestly hadn't believed her former stalker was responsible for the sabotage. "I'm assuming you didn't witness a bank robbery?"

"No."

"Then something you recently said or did might have reminded your saboteur of someone who *was* there, making him think you could ID him."

"But I can't."

"And hopefully by now, he's figured that out. Because if you could, you would have already sent the police after him."

She squirmed. "You really think kids threw those rocks at us back there?'

He narrowed his eyes. "You don't?"

She was more fidgety than a juvenile shoplifter forced to wait for his dad to collect him from the police station. Did she think their elusive bank robber had another reason for coming after her?

Annie expelled a breath through clenched teeth. "I definitely want to believe our rock throwers were kids. But the timing is too coincidental for comfort."

"I agree." He frowned. "But it doesn't make sense."

"What doesn't make sense?"

"The perp coming after you now. The statute of limitations for armed robbery is ten years."

Her attention snapped his way. "You mean it's too late for you to charge him?"

"Exactly. So why would he try to silence you now?"

Annie shuddered but remained silent.

A skin-crawling thought niggled Curt. What if Joey Carmello was the bank robber, and his family had compelled the case detective to compromise the investigation? "Is there something you're not telling me?" Curt prodded, hoping she'd tell him about Carmello herself.

"How am I supposed to know?" Her voice rose defensively. "Maybe I know the guy and don't realize that I know him."

Curt glanced at his watch. "Well, Kai should be at his job soon, and we'll be able to compare his prints to see if he's our man."

"And if he isn't?"

"We keep searching."

Her gaze grew distant, and she shrank into herself. "Where?"

Curt tightened his grip on the steering wheel, his attention shifting in a continuous loop between the road ahead, Annie beside him, and the cars behind. "I don't know yet." The truth was, if the perp was smart enough not to get caught after the robbery, he was smart enough to bide his time. But if Joey had hired him, who knew what he might try next?

Sometimes stalkers became so fixated on the object of their attention that they grew enraged when their plans were foiled. And rage never led to anything good.

Annie opened a map app on her smartphone, then checked a train timetable.

"Please don't tell me you're thinking of running."

She bit her lip. Didn't meet his eyes.

"Annie, don't let this guy scare you into doing something rash."

She bristled. "He's tried to kill me twice. Maybe tried to stone me earlier today. From where I'm sitting, leaving town is a sensible thing to do. Hardly 'rash.'"

The anguish in her voice tore at his heart. "But what if his plan all along has been to lure you into a trap, away from your friends? Away from anyone who could report you missing."

As if sensing Annie's distress, Bella whined.

Annie gripped her phone so tightly, her knuckles whitened. "Why are you doing this to me?"

"I'm trying to keep you safe. That's all. I promise." He glanced in his rearview mirror and spotted the same dark sedan he'd observed when leaving the park, but the distance between them was closing fast. Without signaling, Curt pulled a U-turn.

Bella leaped to her feet with a yelp but struggled to keep her footing.

Annie grabbed the handle above her window and reflexively slammed her foot into the floorboard. "What are you doing?"

"A car's been following us." Curt kept one eye trained on the rearview mirror as he negotiated a sharp right at the next intersection.

The sedan sped past on the other side of the highway without so much as touching his brakes.

Had he misjudged the threat? Or was the guy smart enough to walk away once he'd been made? Might he have an accomplice in a second car?

Curt swerved into a parking lot with a clear view of the highway.

Bella paced the back seat, staring out one window, then the other.

Curt tensed as a yellow Beetle pulled a U-turn at the same point he had. But a moment later, the car parked outside a burger joint, and a teen in a kitchen service uniform climbed out and entered the restaurant. Curt shifted his car into reverse and backed out of his parking space. "Sorry, false alarm."

"You're sure?"

He reached across the console and squeezed Annie's hand. Awareness zinged through him, knocking the air from his lungs with all the force of a bullet to his chest.

The truth was, he couldn't be a hundred percent certain. He stroked his thumb over the back of her hand. "I want to help you," he said softly. "But I need you to trust me." He waited for her to meet his gaze.

"Now, is there anything you haven't told me, no matter how irrelevant it might seem at this moment?"

She ducked her head. "Eight—" She cleared her throat and started again. "Eight years ago, I changed my name and moved to Alaska to—" She clamped her hands on her thighs and swallowed. "To escape a stalker."

"I'm so sorry, Annie," he murmured.

"I don't know how he's found me," Annie rushed on. "*If* he's found me. But if he has, no one around me is safe. He's the son of a mobster—Joey Carmello, part of the infamous Carmello crime family. He's used to getting his way no matter what it takes."

Curt studied the passing cars. Thankfully, none of the drivers appeared to pay attention to them. "Why'd Carmello fixate on you? How did you meet?" His stomach roiled at the possibility that she'd dated the guy.

"I'd come out of a shop on the city's east side when I heard gunfire. An instant later, Joey raced around the corner straight into my path. He stopped me from walking into danger—a drive-by shooting. He was wounded but claimed he'd been a bystander. And I believed him, not that it mattered. I was a nurse. I would've helped him anyway."

"So you saved his life?"

"The wound wasn't that bad. The bullet grazed his leg. I stopped the bleeding and told him he should go to the hospital. My mistake was telling him I worked in the ER." She stared out the windshield. "He told me he didn't want to get mixed up in the investigation. Said anyone brazen enough to gun down a guy in the street wouldn't hesitate to eliminate witnesses."

"So you didn't speak to the police either?"

"No. I didn't witness the shooting, and at the time, I believed him. I'd seen enough trauma victims come through the ER that I understood his fear. And since his wound was superficial, I didn't push. I didn't think I'd ever see him again."

"But he came looking for you at the ER?"

Her breath hissed out with biting self-recrimination. "I was so naive."

"None of this is your fault," Curt insisted.

She continued as if she were so caught up in the memories that she hadn't heard him. "The next day he sent flowers to the ER for me. Two days after that, a box of chocolates. One night, he was waiting outside for me. I didn't offer him any encouragement. I thanked him for the flowers and chocolates but told him they weren't necessary."

Bella stretched her neck over the console between them and rested her head on Annie's arm.

Scratching her dog's ears, Annie continued, "I turned down his dinner invitation. Told him I was dating someone, even though I wasn't." Tears sprang to her eyes. "I never should have—"

Curt squeezed her hand once more. Her fingers were ice-cold. "You did the right thing."

"No. I didn't. He stopped sending me gifts, but he started *coincidentally* showing up at places where I was—the grocery store, the library, a night out at a restaurant with friends, even church."

"Did you tell the police?"

"Tell them what? I knew he must be watching me, but he didn't do anything threatening. He acted surprised to see me, and was always cordial."

"Stalkers are notoriously adept at psychological warfare."

"He certainly was," she said bitterly. "Then one night, he 'ran into me' while I was on a date. Later that night, my date was killed in a hit-and-run."

Curt tightened his hold on her hand. "And you suspected Joey?" No wonder she hadn't wanted to tell him about the guy.

"I did." She pulled free of Curt's grasp and wiped the tears from her eyes. "I told the investigating officer. But as soon as he realized *who* I was accusing, he advised me to cut all ties to the city and move far away, maybe even change my name and profession."

"A cop told you to do that?" Curt was aghast that a member of his profession could do such harm.

"Yes. He said stalking was a hard crime to prove, and throwing organized crime into the mix made my situation a lot dicier. He said the Carmellos had too many minions on the inside—people who could be blackmailed to make sure the system worked to the crime family's benefit. Anyone with loved ones or a career that was important to them could be coerced into doing their bidding."

Curt hadn't personally seen such corruption but was fully aware it existed. And when criminals got too much power, the corruption flourished. "That's when you changed your name and moved to Alaska?"

"Yes." She worked her jaw back and forth, the muscles in her cheek tensing with the action. "The officer told me that, given the warped way guys like Joey thought, the moment I accepted his first 'gift,' I'd bound myself to him. And that if they openly investigated Joey for the hit-and-run or put a restraining order on him, his conduct toward me might get ugly real fast."

She stared at Curt, soul-deep anguish shadowing her eyes. "I'm so sorry. I never should've involved you. If anything happens to Noah because of me—"

"You have nothing to apologize for." He brushed a stray tear from her cheek. "I'll find out where this guy is, and who might work for him." He drew back so he could think clearly. The surest way to guarantee her safety would be to have her move into his guest room. But how could he, with Noah under the same roof?

"You don't understand, Curt. These people have their tentacles everywhere. If you start asking questions, Joey will hear about it. And then he'll come after you."

Curt squared his jaw, once more regretting his earlier call to Chicago PD, but he kept the thought to himself. "Joey isn't the only one with connections, Annie. I'll be careful. But promise you'll trust me and won't run."

She stiffened her spine even as her lip quivered. "What if he threatens Noah?"

Curt's gut twisted, but he carefully schooled his features. "Not going to happen."

"It happens all the time. The cop in Chicago told me so. He told me my best hope of escape was to change my name and get as far away as possible."

"Because he wasn't doing his job," Curt seethed.

"No, because he knew what the Carmellos were capable of." Her voice splintered. "I never should have come back. I should've known Iowa was too close to Chicago."

Curt shifted in his seat to face her and gripped her arms. "Listen to me. You can't let this guy flip your life upside down all over again. For all we know, Carmello has nothing to do with the sabotage at your house, or the incident at the park."

She gulped deep breaths as she struggled to contain the tears glistening in her eyes.

"It's possible Kai is our bank robber," Curt went on. "He would've been a teen at the time, but if he'd never been in trouble before, it would explain why he wasn't a suspect."

"You think so?" A spark of hope filled her voice.

"Given how difficult he's been to find, it wouldn't surprise me."

Annie swiped at a tear. "He does seem like the most logical person to resent me, since I moved into his home."

"It's settled then." Curt backed out of the parking space. "I'll let you know as soon as I uncover anything definitive. In the meantime, promise me you won't let your imagination make things worse than they are."

She shivered. "I'll try."

After finishing her last appointment Monday afternoon, Annie returned her client files to the front desk.

"You look as if you could use a coffee," Ian said from the machine in the waiting room.

"No thanks. I don't need to be any more keyed up than I already am."

"Herbal tea, then?"

"Yes please."

As he fixed her a cup, the images on the wall-mounted TV screen snagged her attention. Ian had set up the infomercial stream so clients could learn more about the clinic while they waited for their appointments. The changing slides showed information about their services, products they offered for sale, and bios of all the staff members, complete with photos.

"Earth to Annie."

Annie jumped at Gayle's voice.

"Sorry, I didn't mean to startle you." Gayle limped closer. "You okay?"

"I don't know," Annie admitted. "I'd hoped this whole nightmare could be chalked up to upsetting Grace's former tenant. But the fingerprint evidence that matched Kai's was from the carbon monoxide detector, and he could've left that when he lived there."

Ian handed her the tea he'd made. "So now what?"

Annie shrugged. Curt was checking into Joey's whereabouts. But Gayle and Ian didn't know about Joey, and Annie preferred to keep it that way. "Unless this guy strikes again, there's not much to go on."

Ian and Gayle exchanged glances. "We think you should stay with us until they catch him."

"I couldn't impose on you like that." Annie hauled down her rising voice. "I'll be fine at home, honestly. The security system goes in today. And I have Bella. Plus, Curt has arranged for himself or another officer to escort me to and from work or wherever else I need to go."

A mischievous gleam lit Gayle's eyes. "Curt, huh?"

"Officer Porter," Annie corrected herself

Gayle chuckled. "I'm teasing. But he's clearly smitten with you. As smitten as that adorable son of his."

Annie's heart hiccupped. The little girl inside her—the girl who'd spent her childhood playing princess and believing in happily ever afters—would have liked to believe Gayle's fairy tale. But Kristie Brooks, the woman Annie had been before fleeing Chicago, was too terrified history would repeat itself. "He's doing his job."

"Whatever you say," Gayle acquiesced, but her smirk said she didn't believe it.

The clinic's infomercial on the big screen cycled back to the clinicians' bios, and Annie stared at the photo of herself. "This is an internal presentation for our clients alone, right?"

"No, it's looping through our website pages," Ian said.

"You put my picture on the website?" Annie's voice rose hysterically.

Gayle squinted at her as if she'd grown antennae. "Of course."

Of course. Annie tamped down the panic-driven lecture welling up her throat. How could they have known the danger? She hadn't so much as breathed Joey's name around them. Never mind that even in

Alaska, she'd always avoided being captured in colleagues' snapshots that inevitably found their way onto social media.

Annie peered at the image of herself. She didn't even remember the photo being taken. She certainly hadn't posed for it. But it had to be how Joey found her—using facial-recognition software. The new name wouldn't have thrown him off once he saw her face.

An infant's cry snapped her from her thoughts. Her attention shifted to the young family entering the clinic—children that might be endangered if Joey came after her there.

Annie shoved the cup of tea back at Ian. "I shouldn't be here."

$\mathcal{I}$gnoring Gayle's pleas to wait for her police escort, Annie rushed out of the clinic. Grace's handyman, Ray Adams, had said he'd wait at the house for her to walk her through the new security system. She'd stop by Grace's to pick up Bella on the way. She would be fine. Officer Porter had more important things to do than escort her to and from work. Once she was home, she'd call and let him know as much.

Curt's car sat in Grace's driveway.

Please don't let Joey have gotten to Grace. Annie swerved into the driveway, dashed up the porch steps two at a time, and burst through the front door without bothering to knock. "Grace? Are you okay?"

"Fine, dear." Grace, Curt, and Bella emerged from the kitchen. "What's wrong?"

"I saw Curt's car and was worried."

Curt's head tilted, his gaze roaming her face, her clenched fists. "I thought I'd fetch Bella before meeting you at your office." The gentleness in his voice made her eyes burn and her throat ache. He smelled like the fresh scent of air after a rain, which was something she should definitely not be noticing.

She glanced at Grace, then back to Curt, trying to ignore the compassion in his eyes. "Sorry, I should've called to let you know I decided to leave early."

"Not a problem."

"Thank you." She didn't want to explain anything further in front of Grace. Annie thanked Grace for dog-sitting and loaded Bella and her bag into the car, then followed Curt to her home, where he did a security sweep while Ray showed her how to use the security system.

"Remember to arm the panel with the 'Stay' button when you're home. That way the siren blares the instant a ground-floor window or door is opened." He pointed to a green button. "Use this to temporarily disable the back door sensor, so you can let your dog in and out. If you forget to push it, a three-beep reminder will sound before the siren rings. But hitting the override button will quickly become second nature."

Lastly, he showed her the small video screen he'd mounted in the kitchen that streamed live feed from two outdoor cameras.

Annie motioned to a fragrant bouquet adorning the kitchen table. "Are those from you?"

"I'd like to take credit. But, no. They were delivered about an hour ago." Ray handed her two sets of new keys and headed for the front door.

"I'll see you out," Curt said, jogging up the stairs after checking the basement.

Annie turned her attention to the bouquet, which even included a sunflower, one of her favorite flowers. At least it used to be. The card read: *Hope these bring sunshine to your day.* It was unsigned. Her heart stuttered.

Joey used to call her his sunshine. And she'd made the mistake of telling him sunflowers were her favorite.

Staring at the sunflower and picturing her image on the clinic's website, she sucked in a breath.

Curt rejoined her in the kitchen. "Annie? What's wrong? You've gone pale."

She blinked. Hearing him say her name with such concern did funny things to her heart. "Um, these wouldn't happen to be from you, would they?"

"The card wasn't signed?" His ominous undertone as he reached for it made goose bumps erupt on her arms.

"No."

"Ah." He passed her the card, his fingers warm and callused. "That sounds like something Grace would say. Give her a call and ask."

Annie immediately retrieved her phone from her purse and pulled up Grace's number. "It's her voice mail," Annie said to Curt, and left a message after the beep.

"If she says she didn't send them, let me know."

"I will." Annie took a deep breath. She had promised not to believe the worst, but it was also dangerous to ignore all the signs that it had happened. "I think I might've figured out how Joey found me, if that's what's going on."

"How?" Curt asked, without attempting to dissuade her.

"The Kemps posted my photo on the clinic website. He could have used software to run a search for my image. I've done it myself with pictures of plants I was trying to identify in my garden in Alaska."

Curt grimaced. "You don't think the name would have made him think twice about the seeming likeness." It wasn't a question.

"I read somewhere that the software pays special attention to the shape and position of the ears, eyes, and nose. Things that can't easily be changed, like cutting and coloring your hair or wearing color contacts."

"Let's not borrow trouble. His name didn't pop up when we ran the prints. And I'm confident they'd be in the database, given his family connections. I've asked a friend in Florida to inquire whether Joey's in the system, to avoid any risk of the request being traced to Iowa. If he is, then it's unlikely he's our culprit."

Annie expelled a relieved sigh. "Thank you. Would you like a cup of tea?"

"I should be going," he said, a hint of apology in his tone. "Sylvie has a meeting tonight, so I can't be late picking up Noah. But don't hesitate to call if you sense any danger."

"I will."

Her voice must have betrayed the fear that had slithered back into her mind at the prospect of being alone, because he added, "Try not to worry. A patrol car will drive by your place hourly."

Annie locked the door after him and armed the security system, then fixed herself supper.

After supper, Gayle called to convince Annie that she couldn't let her patients down by staying away from the clinic. "I promise we will take whatever extra security precautions Officer Porter deems necessary."

Somewhat reassured by Curt's explanation of how the fingerprint search worked and the fact that none of the prints found on her brake line or at her house could be matched to Joey, Annie relented and agreed to return to work.

"Okay, Bella," Annie announced the next morning as she pulled on jeans and a warm sweater. "I don't start work until eleven, so that means you get a nice long walk." She grabbed her keys and switched the alarm panel from *Stay* to *Away*, then bustled Bella out the front door during the sixty-second beeping delay allotted for exit. The escalating urgency of the beep as the seconds ticked down was enough to raise her stress level.

She stood on her porch and scanned the sidewalk, the street, the nearby yards—something she realized she should have done from the safety of her living room window. Annie shortened Bella's leash.

"You'll protect me from strangers, right, girl?" *As long as they aren't savvy enough to carry dog biscuits*, she thought morosely.

Bella tugged.

"All right. Let's go."

Children filtered onto the sidewalks, skipping their way to the elementary school around the next block. Their appearance made her feel safer. Surely whoever was after her wouldn't make a move with so many youngsters about. He couldn't be that heartless.

Several kids asked if they could pet Bella, who happily obliged by giving them high fives and wagging her tail.

Soon, the school bell sounded, and the children dashed off. Annie's trepidation returned with the growing silence. She lifted her chin and lengthened her stride. She wasn't the criminal in the situation. Why should she cower about the streets?

The internal pep talk invigorated her step, and three blocks later, she headed back to the house. As they reached her corner, she cocked her head at an out-of-place sound. *What was that?*

She quickened her steps. Neighbors emerged from their homes, no doubt also wondering about the piercing noise. When her house came into view, Annie's feet began to drag. The pulse raging in her ears almost drowned out the wail of her security alarm.

Then the alarm abruptly stopped.

Annie's stomach clenched. The one other person who knew the disarm code was Grace's handyman, Ray. And his van was nowhere to be seen.

With the sound silenced, her neighbors retreated into their homes before Annie reached her driveway.

Scanning her windows and door for signs of a break-in, she pulled out her phone. A missed call from the security system's auto-dialer appeared on the screen. A lot of good that feature did when she had her phone on silent.

She called Curt.

Seeing nothing amiss at the front of the house, Annie ventured onto the porch and slid her key into the lock. "I'm so glad I reached you," she said when Curt answered. "I don't know what's wrong. The alarm sounded while I was walking Bella, but now it's stopped."

"I'm on my way. I had Ray add my number to the auto-dialer. Where are you now?"

"At the front door." She pushed it open. "The security panel should tell me which sensor tripped."

"Absolutely not. Wait outside."

Something clattered in one of the bedrooms.

Bella dashed in.

"Bella, no!"

Curt flicked on his siren and raced through the streets to Annie's house, shouting her name into his hands-free system.

The answering silence drove his foot to the floorboard. Several minutes later, he barreled into the driveway and slammed the car into park before he'd come to a full stop.

The front door yawned open. No sign of Annie, nor Bella.

He mounted the stairs two at a time and paused at the open door, taking in what he could see of the main floor. Nothing appeared out of place.

A sharp bark sounded from one of the bedrooms.

Hand on the butt of his holstered gun, Curt eased along the interior wall until he had a view of the kitchen and mudroom. Both were clear. No evidence of a scuffle. He cocked his ear toward the bedrooms.

Eerie silence.

He edged down the hall. At the first doorway, he peeked into the room and got walloped.

Drawing his weapon, he staggered to regain his balance and train his gun on his assailant. "Annie?"

Her eyes rounded. She dropped the heavy textbook she was holding, as if it had burst into flames. "I'm so sorry. I didn't realize it was you." She fluttered her hand. "Bella was barking at the ceiling, and then I spotted someone running along the side of the house. I heard the police siren, but then I heard the floorboard creak and thought you were the intruder coming back."

"My fault. I should've announced myself." Curt holstered his weapon. "You saw the intruder?"

"I caught a glimpse. He ran from the side of the house into the backyard and hopped the fence."

Curt glanced in each of the bedrooms. Neither room had a window to the side of the house and none of the windows were open. "Did he run out the front door?" Curt had closed and locked it.

"No, I would've seen him."

Curt still needed to check the rest of the house, but every second he waited before going after the intruder allowed him to get farther away, giving him a better chance of escaping altogether. "You said you saw the person running away. How would you describe him?" When she didn't immediately respond, he prompted with, "Tall, short? Dark hair, light? Skin color? Young, old?"

"White, in his twenties or thirties, maybe? Average height, but thin and lanky. Hair was light, maybe sandy-blond. He wore a bright-orange T-shirt."

Curt's hopes surged. "That should make him easy to spot." He tapped the radio on his shoulder. "All units be on the lookout for a male, fleeing on foot, in the vicinity of Vine and Oak." He related the description Annie had given him, then added, "If found, hold for questioning in connection with a break-in."

Annie stood in the hallway, gaping at him.

"What's wrong?"

She gave her head a shake. "Nothing. I've just never seen you in uniform before. I guess I assumed you were a plain-clothes detective."

"In small-town police departments, we tend to pull double duty." He strode to the kitchen, praying the off-duty officers were listening to their scanners and would keep their eyes open for her intruder, because only one other officer was actually on duty. "Wait here. I'm going to check the basement."

She trailed him to the top of the stairs.

A basement window sat open, and the wires on the security system's sensor hub had been yanked. Curt hurried back upstairs to the aroma of coffee brewing, and Annie filling a plate with muffins. "It looks as if your intruder entered through a basement window. But instead of hauling himself straight back out, he disabled your system."

Her hands trembled as she set a pair of mugs on the counter. "It's that easy?"

"By yanking the wires, he cut off the power from both the battery backup and the electricity, but thankfully he didn't know enough to cut the power to the dialer."

Annie chewed on her bottom lip, clearly not comforted by the detail. "A few neighbors came outside when the siren went off. One of them might've seen the guy."

"I'll speak to them."

Annie swiped at something on the counter. "I swear I don't know where the dust comes from in this house sometimes."

Curt's gaze snapped to the ceiling. "You said Bella was barking at the ceiling."

"Yeah, that's what it seemed like anyway."

He squinted at what, at first glance, he might have mistaken for a fly or other tiny insect on the ceiling, but what actually appeared to be a tiny drilled hole on closer inspection. "Did you hear noise coming from the attic?"

"Not over Bella's barking, no."

But the dog had obviously detected something. "Where else have you noticed an unusual amount of dust?"

Her head tilted, trepidation shadowing her eyes. "Besides here, I'm forever sweeping tiny dust clouds off the end table in the living room, and the top of the washing machine."

Curt peered at the ceiling above the washing machine. A tiny hole had been drilled into it too. Seething at what it meant, he strode into the living room and spotted a third suspicious spot. Fisting his hands, he raced to Annie's bedroom.

Annie trailed after him with Bella on her heels. "What is it?"

To his relief, there didn't appear to be any spy holes in her bedroom ceiling. He squinted about at the pictures on the wall, the contents of the bureau top and shelf—anywhere the creep might hide a camera. Nothing immediately stood out to him, and not wanting to worry Annie, he didn't share that particular concern. He'd have forensics do a sweep for cameras once Annie was outside. He cupped her elbow and walked with her back to the kitchen. "You have three holes that I can see drilled in your ceilings. Until I get into the attic, I can only speculate on their purpose."

Annie's breath caught. "Peepholes?"

"Possibly."

"But if he was up there before now, I would've heard him, surely. Or Bella would have." She shuddered. "Come to think of it, the first night I moved in I heard lots of creaking, but I chalked it up to the wind in the eaves."

"How long have you lived here?"

"Three weeks."

"And when did you first notice the dust?"

"Pretty much from the day I moved in."

That news heartened Curt somewhat. "Then hopefully the holes aren't connected to your intruder."

She busied herself once more at the counter, her hands trembling more than ever. "Would you like a coffee?"

"Sure. But first I want to check the attic. Can you show me where the hatch is located?" He gritted his teeth at the fact he had to ask. He should've checked it Friday night and every night since.

"This way." Annie strode back to the hall. "It's in the ceiling of the empty bedroom across from the bathroom."

Stopping outside the bedroom, Annie pointed to the attic hatch—the size of a small door, the kind that had stairs built into it.

Curt snapped on a pair of latex gloves, then pulled his flashlight from his duty belt.

Bella, who'd remained glued to Annie's side since Curt arrived, stared into the room and whined.

Curt examined the floor beneath the hatch. Two indents indicated where the end of the ladder had rested on the ground, and a couple of pieces of dried dirt held the shape of a shoe tread. "When is the last time you were in here?"

"I haven't been. I had nothing to put there."

"Is the door usually kept closed?"

"No, I keep it open for the light. Bella sometimes romps around in there. I guess I have been in to vacuum a couple of times."

"When was the last time?"

She frowned. "It would have been a week ago Saturday, since I wasn't here to do housework this past weekend."

"Okay, I need you to stay back and keep Bella out of this room. The county's forensics unit might be able to pick up evidence in here that will help us ID this guy." Spotting a rod with a hooked end behind the door, Curt used it to hook the eye nail on the attic hatch and pull it open. As he expected, the stairs unfolded. "As much as I want to get up there and see what your intruder was up to, I don't want to compromise any potential hand- or shoe prints on this ladder." He backed out of the room and shut the door to keep Bella from disturbing any evidence. "How about you pour us that coffee while I call in a forensics team?"

She straightened, seemingly shoring up her courage. "Yes, of course."

Renewed admiration of Annie's strength snuck up on him. He held her gaze, resisting the undercurrent of awareness that passed between them. He'd been distracted by it Friday night when he hadn't thought to check the attic. He couldn't afford to let it happen again.

While she busied herself with the coffee, Curt put in a call. County was bound to balk at his requesting a forensics team on a simple break-in, but given his strong suspicion that the intruder was also their attempted murderer, he intended to get a crew out ASAP. Another woman was not going to fall victim to intruders on his watch.

"Should we send a bomb disposal unit?" the sergeant asked.

Curt's heart tripped. "Yeah, maybe." How had he not considered that the creep might have left a bomb behind before hightailing it out of there? He hurried back to the kitchen. "We need to get out. *Now.*"

12

$\mathcal{A}$nnie raced to the back of her yard, with Curt's explanation echoing in her head. *The intruder might have planted something in the attic.*

Scanning the neighboring yards and treetops, Curt steered her to the cover of the back shed.

"You think he could be out there waiting to shoot me?"

"There's no obvious line of sight that I can see." He motioned toward the north side of the house. "Is that where you saw the intruder?"

"Yes." She pointed to a crab apple tree halfway down the yard, next to the six-foot wooden privacy fence. "He used that tree to hoist himself over the fence."

"Stay here." Curt shoved his toe into the crook of the tree and hoisted himself high enough to inspect the neighbor's yard. Next, he examined the mangled remnants of the hexagonal attic vent littering the ground and the hole in the side of the house where the attic vent should have been. "If I had to guess, your intruder kicked out the attic vent and shimmied down the downspout. Unfortunately, the ground's been too dry to yield any footprints."

He was in professional mode, and she knew she should be grateful, but it felt as if he'd erected a wall between them—the kind of wall she knew too well. She'd used it time and again in the ER to shield herself from becoming too emotionally involved, from caring too much to be able to do her job.

From him, it was both frightening and painful.

His attention shifted back to the hole in her wall. "I have a buddy who's a roofer. Once forensics is done here, I'll ask him to replace the vent for you. He'll be more comfortable working at that height than Grace's handyman." He frowned.

"What is it?"

"Nothing."

"You were thinking something. And if it was about the intruder, I have a right to know."

"You're right," he said. "I was thinking about the holes drilled in your ceiling."

"You think the intruder's been here before? That he drilled them?"

"If he didn't, Grace's handyman might not be completely innocent."

Annie choked on the thought.

"Or he could be entirely blameless," Curt added quickly. "We'll know better once forensics examines the attic."

When the county forensics team arrived, Curt joined them inside, and a female officer kept watch over Annie in the backyard. The time crawled by.

Last night, she might have been happy for the excuse to stay away from work, but the more she'd thought about what Gayle said, the more she knew her friend was right. Her clients depended on her. She couldn't let them down. She couldn't let Joey—or whoever the creep was—win.

For the umpteenth time, she glanced at her watch. "I need to get ready for work. How much longer before I can go back inside?"

"I'll ask," the officer said. A moment later, she received the all clear. No bombs had been left in the attic.

Breathing a little easier, Annie headed inside.

Curt, looking incredibly handsome and formidable in his dark blue uniform, beckoned her into the once-empty bedroom, which was riddled with items sealed in evidence bags—a sleeping bag, clothes, a lantern, a book. None of which belonged to her.

Nausea swirled. "He was living in my attic?"

Curt caught her hand, the warmth of his grounding her. "Please, sit down," he urged, easing her to the floor. "Put your head down for a minute."

Feeling the room spin, she did as he suggested.

"It seems a squatter's been living in your attic. But his fingerprints don't match our bank robber's."

She jerked straight. "They don't?"

"No. Which makes it unlikely he was behind the attacks, especially since stuffing the furnace pipe would have killed him as readily as you."

She shivered, and something softened on Curt's face.

He retrieved a small evidence bag containing a lone nine-volt battery. "He may, however, have inadvertently made the situation worse. We suspect this is the missing battery from your CO detector. Perhaps he pulled it when the detector went off, and when that didn't stop the noise, he went downstairs and opened the breaker."

She stared at the battery. "You're saying he's smart enough to know how to shut off a breaker, but not smart enough to know what the alarm meant?"

"CO is colorless and odorless. Some people don't believe the alarms. They think they're tripping over nothing, like when smoke detectors go off over a little overbrowned toast."

Annie frowned. "If he's been living up there all this time, how did Bella and I not hear him?"

Curt crossed his arms over his chest. "Good question. Maybe he slept here during the day while you were at work, then went out at night. It could explain why you caught him here today. He would've expected you to be at work."

"I'm working a later shift today."

"Right. And this would've also been the first morning he'd have encountered the new security system."

Annie's eyes widened. "The sandalwood smell I noticed the night I went down to the breaker panel. It must have been his." Her gaze snapped to Curt's. "It's got to be Kai."

"Grace's former tenant?"

"It makes perfect sense. He knows the house. Like you said before, he might've kept a copy of the key, so he wouldn't have had any trouble coming and going undetected until he found the locks changed this morning." Annie pushed to her feet, more convinced than ever. "Since Kai lived here for a year, the neighbors wouldn't have thought twice about seeing him at the house."

"That's true." Curt grinned. "I'll have the prints from the attic compared with the ones on file."

Annie wrinkled her nose at Bella. "Some guard dog you turned out to be."

Bella wagged her tail.

"Don't be too hard on her. As a breed, huskies don't tend to concern themselves with guarding property, but they're loyal and will protect their pack." Curt scratched behind Bella's ear. "And Annie is the head of your pack, right?"

Bella vocalized her agreement—or how much she appreciated the ear rub.

Annie glanced at the time. "I need to get to work." She waved an arm at the chaos. "Is it all right if I leave you to this?"

"Yes, but I'll drive you to the clinic."

Annie wanted to tell him it wasn't necessary, but after the morning's scare she wasn't feeling quite that brave. "Give me five minutes to change."

A few minutes later, she grabbed her purse and found Curt at the front door.

When they reached the clinic, Curt walked her to the entrance. "Don't worry about a thing. I'll make sure Bella's locked safely in the house when we're done. And I'll find Kai. He won't bother you again."

"Thank you." She tilted her head and, scrunching her nose, eyed the bruise blooming at his hairline. "I'm sorry I hit you with a book. I should have offered you some ice for that."

He touched his forehead. "I'm fine. Hadn't even thought about it. Take care, Annie."

The tenderness in his voice warmed her, which was unwelcome. She watched him through the glass door as he walked back to his car. The morning's incident may not have been her attacker's handiwork, but she knew he was still out there, watching and waiting. She scanned the area around the parking lot. And if the culprit was one of Joey's men, or anything like him, she shouldn't let herself be seen with Curt. At least not in anything other than an official capacity.

Had her last date's death taught her nothing? When she left Chicago, she'd promised herself to never become attached to anything or anyone that a creep like Joey could hold over her.

Drawing in a deep breath and expelling it slowly, she strode through the building's lobby to the clinic's main door. After years of distancing herself from the emotions of her ER patients to preserve her sanity, it had been easy to extend that same emotional distance to all her new acquaintances and colleagues in Alaska. Perhaps her life wasn't destined for the fairy-tale ending of her childhood dreams, but she had the next best thing—satisfaction in helping others recover their own best lives through physical rehabilitation. And if she kept telling herself that, maybe she'd believe it as much as she had before moving to Iowa and meeting Curt.

An hour later, Curt texted confirmation that the prints from the items found in the attic were a match for Grace's former tenant.

Kai was indeed the squatter.

The news was a relief in a way, but it was crazy to think that she'd had both a squatter in her attic *and* an anonymous bank robber trying to kill her. She shuddered. Could the attempts on her life really have been a case of mistaken identity? And if so, had the criminal realized his mistake yet?

Annie shoved aside the disturbing thoughts and busied herself with her patients for the next several hours.

"There's a call for you on line one," Debbie said when Annie stepped out of the consultation room between appointments.

"I'll take it in my office." Annie grabbed a water bottle from the mini fridge in the break room, then ducked into her office and tapped the speaker button on her desk phone.

"Annie, dear, it's Grace. I'm sorry I didn't get back to you last night. I just saw I had a voice mail from you."

Annie finished swallowing a swig of water. "That's okay, Grace. I wanted you to know how much I appreciate the flowers you sent."

"But I didn't send them." Her voice became silky. "You must have an admirer."

A chill shivered down Annie's spine that had nothing to do with the ice-cold water bottle in her hand. Her mind zigzagged to the peepholes they assumed Kai had drilled through the ceiling. What if they hadn't been merely to allow him to ensure the coast was clear before he crept out of the attic? What if he'd developed some sort of attachment to her? He could have sent the flowers.

And what did it say when, as creepy as that sounded, she'd rather believe Kai sent the bouquet than Joey?

"Listen, Grace, I have to see my next client in a bit, so could you do me a favor?"

"Of course, dear. What do you need?"

"Could you call your handyman and ask him which florist delivered the flowers?" With any luck, she could track down who'd sent them that way.

"I'd be happy to. Or I could save us some time and ask Curt if he sent them," she added teasingly.

"He didn't. I already asked."

"Oh." Grace sounded disappointed by the fact. "Well, isn't that a fine kettle of fish?" She chuckled.

Annie muffled a groan. "I'm not interested in a significant other."

"That does tend to be when they crawl out of the woodwork."

Fish? Crawling? Grace didn't make Annie's supposed potential admirers sound terribly appealing.

"I'd better let you get back to work."

"Wait." Annie's grip on her water bottle tightened. As much as she hated to tell Grace about Kai, Annie would rather the news came from her than someone else. "There's something I have to tell you."

"This sounds serious." All amusement vanished from Grace's tone.

"It is. I'm afraid we discovered this morning that your former tenant has been living in the attic since his lease ended."

"What?" Grace sputtered as if she were choking. "I—I'm so sorry. This is my fault. I should've made sure he had another place to stay." She made a sad sound. "Officer Porter doesn't think Kai sabotaged the furnace, does he?" Her voice broke. "This is horrible. He must've thought he could get the rental back if—if something happened to you."

"Please don't think that. The evidence suggests he may have come close to being a victim himself."

"Oh, dear." Grace's voice was unsteady.

"His prints definitely don't match the bank robber's prints found on my brake line." Annie offered a few more reassurances, then ended the call, wishing she hadn't had to give Grace such news.

She collected her next patient's file from the holder on the door of the consultation room, but when she pushed the door open, the room was empty. "Debbie, do you know where Bernie Dyball is? He's not in the exam room."

Debbie covered the receiver of the phone tucked under her ear. "Yes, he dashed out. Said something about an emergency call. This call is also for you. Do you want to take it here or in your office?"

"Who is it?"

"A Mrs. Smith."

Annie frowned. "A patient?"

Debbie spoke into the phone. "May I ask the reason for your call?" Once again, she covered the receiver with her palm. "She's found your dog."

"My dog?" Had Bella escaped with the police going in and out of the house, without anyone realizing? Annie snatched the phone from Debbie. "This is Annie."

"Hi, dear," the woman on the other end of the line said, her voice sounding crackly from age but decidedly unthreatening. "I caught your adorable husky."

Annie's breath hitched. "Is she okay?"

"Yes, seems to be. She's a sweet thing. I found your name and number on her tag. Can you come pick her up?"

Annie glanced at her watch. With Bernie's cancellation, her next client wasn't due for twenty-five minutes.

"I need to be off, so you must come right away," the woman added. "I wouldn't want her to break loose again and get run over or something."

"No, of course I'll come now. What's your address?" Annie jotted down the information the woman rattled off. "Thank you. I'll be there in a few minutes." Annie handed the phone back to Debbie. "Is Ian with a client?"

"Yes."

"What about Gayle?"

"She is too."

Annie deflated.

"Can I help?" Debbie asked.

"Would you mind if I borrowed your car? My dog got loose, and I have to pick her up. Someone dropped me off for work."

"Sure. No problem." Debbie handed Annie the keys. "It's parked on the east side of the building."

"Thanks." As Annie hurried out, she scanned the parked cars in the lot and surrounding area, taking some comfort in the fact that Joey, or whoever was after her, wouldn't be looking for her in a black SUV.

Once inside the vehicle, Annie headed for the address the woman had given her. At each turn, she watched her rearview mirror to ensure no one had followed her.

She steered onto Pine Street and shivered at the *No Exit* sign. Scanning the house numbers, she rode the brakes down the street—thirty-eight, forty. Only two houses remained, but the woman had said her house number was fifty. Annie's fingers tightened around the steering wheel, and her heart hammered.

She'd been duped.

Annie mentally kicked herself for being taken in so easily by the elderly voice. If she'd thought about what the woman had said for two seconds, she would've realized it was all a ruse. The clinic's phone number wasn't even on Bella's dog tag—Annie's cell phone number was.

Annie squinted into the trees beyond the street's dead end. Joey was bound to be hiding there, waiting for her. But with any luck, he hadn't figured out she was driving Debbie's SUV. Annie threw it into reverse and swung her arm over the back of the seat to back up.

A black pickup drove straight at her.

She was trapped.

Curt stepped on the gas. "Come on, pick up, pick up," he yelled at his phone after taking the call from Annie's boss. What had Annie been thinking, going out after Bella on her own? Thank goodness the receptionist had a GPS location service on her SUV.

Annie's voice mail picked up his call.

Curt canceled the call and phoned the receptionist back. "Is your vehicle still on Pine?"

"Yeah, it hasn't moved."

Curt's skin crawled. He didn't know whether to be relieved or worried. Annie could've already been snatched, and the SUV abandoned. "Hang on, Annie. I'm coming."

Dispatch called him on the radio. "Officer confirms the victim's dog is still in her house."

"Roger that." Curt slapped the steering wheel. He knew it had to be a setup. Someone was bent on terrorizing Annie, and he still had no idea who or why.

Curt wheeled onto Pine Street as a dark SUV executed a sharp U-turn at the dead end. He swerved to block the vehicle's escape.

The driver's eyes locked with Curt as her brakes squealed. *Annie.*

Curt jumped from his vehicle and, using it as cover, scanned the area for threats. At the sight of a man emerging from a black pickup, Curt drew his gun.

The man tossed a glance their way, then proceeded up the driveway toward a house.

Annie sat frozen, her fingers clamped around the steering wheel.

Curt cautiously rounded his vehicle, hyperalert for trouble as a couple of homeowners stepped onto their porches and peered in his direction. The instant he opened Annie's door, she launched herself at him.

"You came." Her arms circled his middle, and she buried her face against his chest. "How did you know where to find me?"

The mix of fear and relief in her voice matched the erratic thud of his heart. He pressed his cheek to the top of her head. Her hair smelled like apple blossoms in springtime. He flattened his palm against her back to still her trembling. "Debbie connected me to the vehicle's GPS."

"I'm sorry. I was so worried about Bella. I didn't even suspect the call could have been a trap."

His heart clenched. If he'd been any later—

He shut down the thought and swallowed the emotion that welled unbidden in his throat. "Did you see anyone?"

"No," she said, her voice muffled against his shirt. "I realized I'd been duped when the house numbers didn't fit what I'd been told. But the instant I went to back out of the street, the pickup pulled in behind me and I thought it was—I mean, I panicked."

"Shh," Curt soothed. "You're safe now."

She lifted her head to meet his gaze. "But for how long?"

Something inside him shifted at her watery eyes, the desperation in her voice. He swept a strand of hair from her face and stroked his thumb across her chin. "We're going to figure this out and stop this guy. Meanwhile, Bella is home, safe and sound." He urged her to climb back into the SUV. "Park at the curb for a few minutes while I check the end of the road and see if I can find evidence of who might've been waiting for you."

Annie checked the clock on the dash. "I have to get back to the clinic for an appointment."

"Phone in. Let the receptionist know you'll be there soon."

Annie swallowed hard. "Yes. Okay."

Curt locked her door before closing it, then drove to the end of the street. The ground was littered with wind-strewn garbage, and an abundance of footprints and animal tracks heading toward a wooded trail that carried on after the road ended. There was no way of knowing which, if any, of the debris or prints were connected to Annie's caller.

A man ambled down his driveway toward Curt. "What's going on?"

"Have you noticed anyone suspicious hanging about here in the last half hour or so?"

"No. I got back from walking my border collie on the trail a little while ago. We didn't pass a soul."

"Good to know. Thank you. I think it's a false alarm." What was Annie's tormentor playing at? Why would he lure her to a street with no apparent plan?

Knowing she had clients to see, Curt didn't get out of his car after following Annie back to the clinic. "I'll be here by eight to drive you home," he said out his window. With any luck, he'd have Kai in custody long before then.

When the BOLO on Kai turned up nothing all day, Curt resorted to staking out his workplace after supper. The young man wasn't scheduled to work until eleven, but his boss revealed that Kai often arrived early and hung around until his shift started. Shortly after six, Curt spotted Kai—sporting a navy hoodie over his bright-orange T-shirt—walking toward the convenience store. Curt leaped from his car. "Kai Aldred, I need to ask you some questions."

Kai took off across the street, and Curt sprinted after him. Kai ducked behind the diner, clambered over a fence, and loped across the park. Staying tight on his heels, Curt radioed for backup. "East entrance, Main Street Park. No lights or siren." To Kai, he said, "Kai, why are you running? I just want to talk. Running makes you seem guilty."

Kai stumbled at that indictment, recovered but continued at a slower pace.

Rather than overtake him, Curt matched Kai's pace. "*Are* you guilty of something?"

"No." Still running, but more erratically now, Kai covered his head with his arms.

"Then stop for a minute," Curt said. "Let's talk. Okay?"

Kai continued his slowing lope, as Curt edged him toward the east entrance.

A moment later, a squad car squealed to a stop twenty yards in front of them.

Kai skidded to a stop, and his hands shot into the air. "I didn't do anything wrong. I didn't."

"Let's go to the station, and you can explain what your stuff was doing in Annie Bishop's attic." Curt handcuffed Kai and helped him into the waiting squad car. Deciding to pick up his car later, he caught a ride to the station with Officer Bacon.

But back at the station, when Curt laid out all the evidence, Kai continually shook his head and repeated, "I didn't do anything wrong. I didn't do anything wrong."

Curt tried a new tact. "Given the facts I've presented, you are also under suspicion for two counts of attempted murder."

Kai's face blanched, his eyes widening to the size of baseballs. "It wasn't me. I never hurt anyone."

"But you have been sleeping in the attic at the current residence of Ms. Annie Bishop."

"It was my place first. Grace shouldn't have kicked me out."

"So you tried to scare the new tenant into leaving town by luring her to a dead-end street?"

"I don't know what you're talking about."

"Where were you this afternoon?"

"Near the hydroelectric dam, sleeping under a tree."

Curt signaled to his colleague through the one-way mirror to see if he could verify the info. "Back to the house. How did you enter the premises after your lease expired?"

"I have a key. Well, had one, until Ray changed the locks. I was there when he did it. I watched through the peephole. But when he was busy getting the flowers from the delivery guy, I snuck out of the attic into the basement and out a window, leaving it unlocked so I'd have a way to get back in this morning. I didn't know he was putting an alarm in too."

"Did you have the flowers delivered to distract him?"

Kai gaped at him. "What? No. I don't even have a phone. How would I do that?"

"How did you come and go from the house without Ms. Bishop knowing?"

"I sleep there during the day when she's at work, then leave before she gets home. On the weekends, I camp out in the park, but soon it'll be too cold to do that."

"Now, this is very important," Curt said. "Were you there Friday afternoon, when someone else came to the house?"

"You mean the meter reader?"

Curt leaned closer. "That's right. What can you tell me about him?"

"I couldn't see him that well, because he wore a dark hoodie. I came down to see what was going on because the dog was going nuts, but I knew it was too early for Annie to be home."

"And he was near the water meter?"

"I guess. He was hunched over right by the wall at the back of the house. I had to look at a sharp angle just to see him from the kitchen window."

Curt's pulse quickened at Kai's description of the location of the furnace pipe. He didn't recall seeing a water meter there. "Can you describe the guy?"

"He was stooped over, but I don't think he was as tall as me. He had a small build."

"Could he have been a teen?"

"Sure. I guess."

"Notice anything else about him?"

"Nah." Kai pressed his palms on the table. "Am I in trouble because I let the dog out? I didn't mean to. The meter reader made me late leaving. I had to rush out the back, and the dog slipped out."

"Why'd you take the battery out of the CO monitor?"

"The what?"

"The device plugged into the outlet in the hall."

"Oh. It was chirping when I got home Friday morning and was driving the poor dog nuts." Kai's explanation mirrored Curt's theory. "I meant to grab a new battery from the store to change it."

A knock sounded at the door, and Officer Bacon poked his head into the room. "There's a call for you. She says it's urgent."

Curt's pulse spiked. He surged to his feet and strode out of the room. "Ms. Bishop?"

"No, it's Grace Kemp."

Curt grabbed the desk phone. "Grace, what's wrong?"

"Annie told me Kai was living in the attic of my rental."

"That's right."

"Well, I don't want to press charges."

"It's a little more complicated than that."

"Then uncomplicate it." Her tone, utterly not Grace-like, brooked no argument. "It's my fault he was left homeless. I had no idea he hadn't found another place. You can bring him here to my house. He can stay in the room over my garage until we can find another place he can afford."

"That's good of you," Curt said. He had already sensed that Kai didn't pose a threat to anyone. "I can have someone deliver his belongings there shortly, but he won't show up himself until after his shift ends tomorrow morning."

"That's fine with me," Grace said, sounding like her cheery self once again. "Before I let you go, did Kai happen to take credit for sending those flowers Annie received?"

"No, he didn't."

"It's so strange to have no idea who sent them. I tried calling Ray, my handyman, several times to ask which shop made the delivery so we could trace the sender, but Ray hasn't returned my calls. And that's not like him at all. Would you mind stopping by his place to make sure he's all right?"

"I can do that." If he didn't hurry, he'd be late meeting Annie. "I've got to go. See you soon with Kai's stuff."

After finishing with her last client of the evening, Annie retreated to her office to finalize her notes. Noticing movement in the hall, she hurried to the door to see if Curt had arrived to escort her home.

"Hi, Sylvie. What are you doing here so late?"

Sylvie bobbed the stack of shoeboxes she was carrying. "Delivering this week's special orders. Noah has Kids' Klub at the church tonight, so I figured it was the perfect time to put a dent in my to-do list. I've gotten a little behind with the extra hours Curt has needed me to watch my nephew."

Annie winced, knowing her troubles were responsible for tying up so much of Curt's time.

"You two about ready to leave?" the receptionist called from the front. "I'm getting ready to lock up."

"Be right out," Annie said, then excused herself from Sylvie to shut down her computer and gather her things.

When she reached the front desk, she asked Debbie, "Is Officer Porter here yet?"

Debbie motioned to the lobby as she switched off the back hall lights. "Coming in now."

"Perfect timing." Annie waved to him, then held up a single finger to signal she'd be a moment. She poked her head into Ian's office to thank him for sticking around, but the lights were already off. "Ian left?"

"No, he's helping Sylvie carry in more boxes—samples of her new fall collection."

Spotting Curt holding the main door for them, Annie hurried out.

"Could you pick Noah up tonight?" Sylvie asked Curt. "I still have two more stops to make."

Curt glanced at his watch, then at Annie. "We'd have to swing past the church before I see you home. Is that okay?"

"Of course." Annie wanted to tell him she could ask Ian to drive her home, but she wanted to hear what Kai had to say for himself. She hoped he'd taken credit for that afternoon's crank call, which resulted in her wild goose chase.

"I can take care of these." Ian added the boxes Sylvie was carrying to his own and urged her to go on to her next delivery.

"Thanks. I'll come by another day to arrange a display," Sylvie said. "Debbie seems anxious to be off."

"No problem."

Curt and Ian talked for a few moments, then Annie and Curt also exited. Darkness shrouded the parking lot. But with Curt at her side, Annie felt remarkably at ease. The air was mild and still—a beautiful autumn evening.

Sylvie braked at the exit and waved to them.

Then, out of nowhere, a loud crack of sound erupted.

14

The ground smothered Annie's scream as Curt pushed her down and shielded her with his body.

But the gunshots stopped as abruptly as they'd started.

Sylvie slammed on her horn. Was she hit? Where was the shooter?

"Stay down," Curt ordered her, drawing his weapon.

Annie scrambled closer to the building. She hated to cower inside while he faced the unknown. Police officers had to be wired differently, somehow. Because when everyone else was running from trouble, they headed straight for it. She ought to know. As an ER nurse, she'd treated the fallout of such disregard for their personal safety far too many times to count. She breathed a prayer for Curt's protection.

Ian pushed open the lobby door.

"Stay inside," Curt shouted, dashing to Sylvie's car in a crouch. He tapped her passenger window and peered through. "You okay?"

Sylvie released her horn. But with Ian pulling Annie into the building, she didn't hear Sylvie's response.

"Did you call 911?" Annie asked Ian, trying to peer out the window without making herself a target.

The wail of a distant siren punctuated his confirmation. "It sounded like firecrackers going off."

Firecrackers? The way the sound had ricocheted off the building, Annie wasn't sure where the popping sounds originated, or what caused them.

A cruiser careened to a stop on the street, blocking Sylvie's car from leaving.

Curt spoke with the officer who leaped from the car, then escorted his sister to the entrance. "Everyone stay here until we figure out what's going on." Curt and the other officer disappeared around the building.

Seeing Sylvie visibly shaken, Annie realized she, too, was trembling. "Did you see the shooter?" Annie asked Sylvie.

"No. I figured ramming my horn would attract more attention than he'd want and scare him off." She scowled. "Of course, that means he's probably long gone, and they'll be no closer to finding out who this guy is."

"I told you and Gayle I shouldn't be coming into work until they catch this guy," Annie said to Ian. "We're putting patients at risk."

"Let's wait to see what the officers find," Ian cautioned.

A few minutes later, the second officer drove off and Curt, his scowl darker than his sister's had been, joined them in the lobby. "It was kids messing with firecrackers."

"I thought that was what it sounded like," Ian said.

Sylvie's fingers seemed to tighten around her folded arms. "Did you actually see kids?"

"No. But we found the remnants of the firecrackers in the back lot."

"So Annie's stalker could've set them off to scare her. He could've been watching for her to come out, then ran off after he set them."

"I don't think so."

"How do you know?" Sylvie's voice rose exponentially. "She's attracting trouble everywhere she goes. You know what? Believe what you want. I've got to go pick up Noah."

"I said I would," Curt reminded her.

"Not with Annie along. Her stalker could follow you."

Annie shrank back. "She's right."

"No, she's not. I'm trained to detect a tail." Curt motioned to the parking lot. "This was kids messing around. A guy who's made two attempts on a woman's life isn't likely to deescalate to mere firecracker pranks."

"He would if he's out to terrorize her," Sylvie countered, her tone caustic. "Have you forgotten the rock-throwing incident?"

"That's enough," Curt said with such force that his sister fell silent. Then he lowered his voice to scarcely more than a whisper. "You go pick up Noah, and I'll be home shortly."

"I'm truly sorry, but you understand Noah's well-being has to come first, right?" Sylvie asked Annie.

"Of course."

After Sylvie left, Ian excused himself. "I better check on Debbie. I told her to wait in the office when I heard the firecrackers. I think I'll call our past clients too. Maybe one of them saw who was skulking about."

"You didn't see anyone when you were helping my sister carry her boxes?" Curt asked.

"No," Ian said. "And I guess that was already after our patients left. I think we need to mount a few security cams around the building and see who we can pick up."

"Good idea," Curt agreed, then turned his full attention to Annie. "Are you okay? I didn't hurt you when I shoved you to the ground, did I?"

She smiled, remembering the protective warmth of his arms. "Not at all. Thank you for what you did."

Dimples winked in his cheeks as his warm gaze held hers.

She felt absurdly heartened that he didn't respond with a glib, "just doing my job." Somehow it had felt like more than that. Which probably showed how very tired she was. Because it wasn't as if he would let himself care for a woman with a target on her back, not when he had a son to protect.

Not that she was interested in a relationship anyway, so why was she even thinking that way?

Before driving her home, Curt reiterated his certainty that the firecracker episode had been nothing more than another prank. "I sincerely don't think you working at the clinic is endangering anyone."

Annie hoped he was right. Every fiber of her being longed to hop on the next plane out of state, but then, like Gayle had said, the next time Joey found her, she'd have no one watching out for her. Could the bank robber really have no connection to Joey? And was he behind the rock throwing, the crank call, and the firecrackers? Or was Kai?

How could someone coincidentally have so many bad things happen to them in such a short amount of time?

Then again, if two attempts hadn't been made on her life, she probably wouldn't have thought much about the lesser incidents, except to blame them on kids getting up to mischief.

Over a cup of cocoa half an hour later, Curt relayed a play-by-play of his interrogation of Kai. "He didn't take responsibility for anything aside from squatting in the house, drilling holes in the ceiling to monitor when it was safe to leave, and accidentally leaving Bella outside Friday afternoon."

Annie belatedly wondered if Colin Mitchell could've made the crank call but decided that wasn't a possibility she wanted to put on Curt's radar. When Curt relayed a description of the guy Kai had seen in her backyard, Annie thought of Bernie. She wasn't sure why. She had several small-framed male patients with a slight stoop. But Bernie had been the last one she saw Friday afternoon. And he'd left in a huff. She'd actually been surprised that he'd kept his next appointment.

But he hadn't kept it, had he?

According to Debbie, he'd been seated in the consultation room next to Annie's office when Annie took Grace's call. But then he'd hightailed it out of the clinic before she finished talking to Grace.

What if he overheard her tell Grace about the fingerprint matching a bank robber's?

Annie couldn't very well accuse Grace's friend based on nothing but the flimsiest of circumstantial evidence. If Curt questioned the man, the stress alone might spark a heart attack or something. Annie couldn't do that to Grace.

Annie circled her finger around the rim of her cocoa cup. Perhaps she could do one better and eliminate him as a suspect by giving Curt something with Bernie's fingerprints to compare.

"Hey Sylvie," Curt said into the phone as he pulled out of Annie's driveway. "I'm sorry about earlier. I appreciate you staying late with Noah for me. I have one more stop to make."

"Annie's case again?"

"No, Grace asked me to do a wellness check on a friend. Shouldn't take more than ten minutes." With the firecracker incident, he'd almost forgotten about his promise to Grace. And Sylvie didn't need to know that the surveillance he'd left to conduct, right after dinner, had been connected to Annie. He was eternally grateful for the flexibility of his sister's schedule. Although he suspected she'd be less inclined to help him out if he were asking her to babysit Noah so he could go on a date.

He started at the notion. In the five years since his wife's murder, he'd never given so much as a passing thought to dating again. And the fact that Annie had kindled the idea should raise warning flags for so many reasons, not the least of which was that she was the victim in an ongoing investigation.

He tightened his grip on the steering wheel, recalling the panic he'd seen in her eyes after he shielded her from what they thought was gunfire. If he hadn't needed to get home to Noah, he wouldn't have hesitated to pass the night parked in her driveway to keep an eye on her place.

A horn blared, jerking him out of his thoughts. At the green traffic light, he stepped on the gas. He couldn't let his attraction to Annie become a distraction.

He parked at the curb in front of Ray's house, happy to see the man's utility van parked in the driveway. The house was dark, except for a single light burning at the back, so Curt bypassed the front door and headed down the driveway to rap on the back door.

No response.

He knocked again, listening for movement.

Nothing.

Cupping his hands around his eyes, Curt peered through the translucent panel window to the side of the door. Was that a pair of legs sprawled on the floor, sticking out from behind the kitchen counter?

He tried the door. *Unlocked.* His senses heightened as he slowly pushed it open. "Mr. Adams, Safe Haven Police. Are you all right?"

No answer.

"I'm coming in." Curt listened for evidence of an intruder. Hearing nothing, he moved silently toward the man on the floor.

As soon as he saw the man's ashen face, he knew that he was too late. Bracing himself against the roiling in his stomach, Curt crouched next to the body and checked for a pulse anyway, but it was cold.

Curt scanned the room. There was no sign of a struggle, nor obvious signs of trauma, aside from a long, narrow mark at his temple that Ray could've gotten by hitting the countertop as he fell.

Curt called it in, requesting the medical examiner, then texted Sylvie that he'd be much later after all.

Numbness crept over him as he stepped outside to wait for the ME. As a cop, he'd seen his fair share of wellness checks end with an unfortunate outcome. But he hadn't been prepared for it tonight. Although Ray might be well past the age most men would retire, he'd seemed to have the energy and vitality of someone half his age.

Doc Griff, the ME, arrived within twenty minutes, his mouth set in a grim line. "What are we looking at?"

"It's Ray Adams."

Doc's eyebrows lifted. "A burglary?"

"I don't think so. To be honest, once I realized he was dead and determined there were no obvious signs of a struggle, I got out of there. I think he fell and hit his head. Maybe had a heart attack?"

"Okay, let's check it out." Doc crouched next to Ray's body and methodically conducted his assessment, while Curt did a cursory sweep of the rest of the house to rule out the possibility Ray had surprised an intruder.

When Curt returned to the kitchen, Doc said, "Time of death appears to be twenty-four to thirty hours ago." He studied Ray's form once more. "Signs suggest the cause of death is likely due to asphyxiation. However, there is no external evidence that he was strangled, and I can't see any evidence of choking to death. An autopsy will tell me more."

"What about suffocation?"

"It's a possibility."

"So we need to treat this as a crime scene?"

Doc sat back on his heels. "I'm afraid so. Yes."

Curt called the chief to alert him.

"We'll have to hand this case over to the county PD to investigate.

We don't have the manpower to handle a murder investigation," the chief said glumly. "I'll make the call."

"Understood." Truth be told, Curt was relieved. He needed to focus on tracking down Annie's attacker and Joey Carmello, and any possible connection between the two of them.

"Porter," Doc growled. "You're gonna want to see this." He drew Curt's attention to a note tucked beneath Ray's left shoulder.

It was written in all caps, in blue ink, on a scrap of white paper. In its current position, few words were visible, but one of them was clear—*Annie.*

Curt swallowed hard to clear the sound of his pulse hammering in his ears.

Doc lifted the shoulder enough for Curt to read the entire note. The words swept an arctic chill through Curt's chest.

He was in your house. No other man belongs in your house but me, Annie.

Annie woke to the sound of Bella's whining and squinted at the clock. It wasn't like Bella to ask to go out before the sun was up. Annie shoved her feet into slippers and trudged toward the door. "I guess this'll teach me to not forget to leave your supper out for you when I work late, huh?"

Except Bella wasn't sitting at the back door, as she usually did if she needed to go out. Her nose was poked between the living room window curtains.

Annie tensed. "What is it, girl?" she whispered. The security panel by the door confirmed that no sensors had been breached. Annie started toward the curtain to peek outside but thought better of it and studied the camera monitors in the kitchen instead. A sedan sat in her driveway. Annie squinted at the screen. In the predawn light, it was impossible to make out the color, but there was no mistaking that someone occupied the driver's seat. Her pulse quickened.

She snatched up her phone and called Curt.

He answered on the first ring, at the exact moment the person in the car brought his hand to his ear.

"Are you sitting in my driveway?" she blurted, straining to rein in her racing heartbeat.

"Yes."

"Why? You should be home. With your son." She refrained from telling him he'd scared the living daylights out of her. He'd probably use it as further justification for playing bodyguard. Not that she didn't appreciate his chivalry.

"May I come in?" His voice sounded husky, as if she'd woken him.

"Of course." She disconnected the call and went to the door to let him in.

Curt dragged himself up the stairs, his uniform rumpled as if he'd slept in it. Though the dark circles under his eyes indicated that he hadn't slept much.

"What's going on?" she asked, suddenly breathless at the realization that, contrary to the assurances he'd given her the night before, he'd actually thought she needed a bodyguard.

He flinched, as if the sound of her voice physically hurt. "How about a coffee? And then I'll explain why I'm here."

She blinked. The *why* was obvious, wasn't it? To keep her safe. Or had he tracked down her attacker? Or Joey? Her heart thumped.

"Okay?" Curt prodded.

"Yes. Have a seat. I'll put the coffee on." A few moments later, she joined him at the table as the coffee brewed. Bella plopped on the floor beside Curt and rested her head on his knee.

Curt scratched behind her ears. "First of all, I wasn't parked in your driveway all night, as I think you assumed."

"Oh."

"I arrived about fifteen minutes ago. And impressively, this gal kept her eye on me from the moment I drove up."

Annie ruffled Bella's coat. "You watch out for me, huh, girl?"

"She does, though I was surprised she didn't bark. She might have if I'd approached the house."

"She was whining. I assumed she wanted to go out, and I'd ignored her longer than I should have." Annie surged to her feet and brought milk and sugar to the table, then poured the coffee.

"So, what brings you around so early?" She scanned his rumpled uniform. "Looking like you never went home."

"I'm afraid I have sad news." The compassion in Curt's tone cut Annie off at the knees.

Clutching the table edge, she dropped into her chair. "Is it Grace?"

"No, no." His warm hand closed over hers. "It's Ray. Grace had been trying to get hold of him and became worried when he didn't return her calls. She asked me to check on him."

Annie's heart thumped. "What happened?"

"He was dead."

Annie blinked rapidly. "That's awful. Was it a heart attack?"

"We won't know until after the autopsy, but there's evidence to suggest foul play."

Annie felt as if the air had been sucked from her lungs. She wasn't Ray's next of kin. She wasn't even a friend. She hardly knew the man. Which had to mean the reason Curt felt compelled to break the news to her so gently was because the man's death had something to do with her. She struggled to find her voice. "And you think his death is connected to me, somehow?"

Aside from the twitch of a muscle in his jaw, his expression remained neutral. But his hand tightened around hers, betraying his concern perhaps more than he'd wanted.

Curt cleared his throat. "The ME estimates that Ray died soon after returning home Monday evening, which makes you one of the last people to see him alive."

She jerked back. "You can't think I'm a suspect."

"No, not at all. But given the attacks against you and the fact that Ray put in the security and new locks afterward, we'd be remiss not to explore a possible connection."

"Remiss?" Annie narrowed her eyes. Why did she get the feeling he was using police-speak to mask something awful? "You didn't show up at my doorstep before dawn because you'd be 'remiss' not to inform me of Ray's death. What aren't you telling me?"

"I'm not at liberty to discuss Ray's case. All I can say is that it's being treated as suspicious, so the chief has asked the county PD to handle the investigation, since we don't have enough staff to handle a mur— a manpower-intensive investigation."

"A murder investigation," she corrected.

He nodded.

"Do you have any idea who killed Ray? You think it was the guy who tried to kill me, don't you?"

"It will be an avenue they'll explore."

She gritted her teeth at his continued use of cop talk. "Is Joey behind this? Is that what you aren't telling me?"

"I'm not saying that." He searched her gaze, his own unreadable, though his inner turmoil was palpable. After a long silence, he drained his coffee. "For today, I'll drive you to the clinic and pick you up again after work. Ian will have your back while you're there. Then we'll reassess. Maybe Gayle and Ian wouldn't mind having you stay with them for a few days."

"I can't make anyone else a potential target."

Curt let it go, but she could read in his eyes that his mind was already sifting through other options.

Once Curt had Annie safely at the clinic under Ian's watchful eye, he enlisted every available staff member in contacting all the florists within a twenty-mile radius to figure out where Annie's flower delivery originated from, and hopefully who had placed the order.

Adams might have been seen receiving those flowers on Annie's behalf, and it was likely what got him killed.

And what if the killer saw Kai going in and out of the house? He could be next. And now he's at Grace's, which puts her in danger too.

Curt contacted the county PD detective heading up the homicide investigation and floated his theory about the flower delivery connection. "I've got our people trying to track down the florist that delivered them."

"Good," Detective Blake said. "Keep me apprised of any developments."

"In the meantime, could you assign a surveillance team to Grace Kemp's house? If Ray's killer goes after Kai, it might be your best chance of nabbing him." And no way did Curt want Grace or Kai caught in the crossfire.

"Yes, we should be able to spare an officer to keep an eye on the place."

"Great." Curt gave him Grace's address, then called his buddy in Florida to find out what he'd learned about Joey Carmello.

"Didn't you get my text?" his friend asked. "I sent it yesterday morning."

"I must've missed it. I was dealing with a home invasion most of the day." Curt scrolled through the messages on his phone. "Nope, I don't see it."

"Oh. It's showing 'not sent' on my phone. Sorry, it's been crazy here too, or I would've followed up with a call." The sound of a car door slamming and an engine starting sounded over the phone. "I'm putting you on speaker, but I'm alone in my car."

"What did you find out?"

"Good news for your victim. Joey Carmello disappeared six years ago. The rumor is his family bumped him off."

Curt's heart slammed against his ribs. "Are you serious?"

"That's what the lieutenant said. And I did a background check on the lieutenant too. I'm convinced he wasn't spinning me a yarn."

Curt tapped a few keywords into an Internet search engine to find corroboration. "Why would Joey's family take him out?" As much as it was the best news Curt could've hoped for, it didn't make sense with the note the ME found under Ray's body. Because if Joey hadn't written it, who did?

"Apparently, Joey Carmello had an obsessive personality that caused the family a truckload of problems."

Curt scrolled through screen after screen of hits but couldn't find a single mention of Joey's demise. "The lieutenant said he disappeared, not that he died. Could he have scored witness protection for informing on his family?" Curt's skin crawled at the thought of what Joey might've done with the free time he would've had on his hands if he'd had to cut ties with his family and friends. "Was his body ever found?"

"No, it wasn't. But I had the same thought and checked the court docket. Joey's not on it." A siren blared over the phone. "Hey, sorry. I've got to go. I'll catch you later." He hung up before Curt could thank him for the intel.

Part-time officer Bev Young hurried to his desk, waving a paper. "We've got a hit. Flowers by Flora, a shop twenty minutes north of town, has taken credit for the bouquet. The owner said the arrangement was ordered late Sunday afternoon."

"Got a name?"

"No. The purchaser paid cash and didn't leave a name. A college student handles the shop on Sundays, so the owner passed along the student's cell phone number if we want to try to reach her." Bev handed him the information. "Want me to make the call?"

"That's okay. I'll do it. Good work."

For the next two hours, Curt's attempts to contact the student went straight to voice mail. It was his luck that she'd be the studious sort who powered off her phone while in classes. Although, in case she'd ignored his calls because his number wasn't in her contacts, he texted her a brief explanation of why he needed to talk to her ASAP and provided the station's number so she could look it up to verify it was legitimate.

Twenty minutes later, the young woman called him on the station's landline.

"Thanks for getting back to me. Are you able to remember anything about the purchaser of the bouquet I described?"

"Sorry, no. I took a lot of orders on Sunday."

"But these were sunflowers. They must be a unique request."

"Not this time of year. Most of the mixed arrangements include a sunflower or two."

"They were for delivery to Safe Haven, and the buyer paid cash."

"I had at least three cash orders for delivery."

"Can you recall anything at all about the purchasers?" Curt gripped his pen, primed to jot down the information.

"There was a cute guy with an Aussie accent, dark hair. There was a mom and her son. And there was a silver-haired man, whose ramrod posture made me think he must've been in the army." She went silent.

"That's all of them?"

"All I can remember."

Thanking the student, Curt studied the list she'd given him. None were an obvious match to Kai's description of the guy he saw in Annie's yard, which may or may not be their anonymous bank robber or Ray's killer.

Curt jotted *Who could have seen Ray at Annie's house?* across the top of a piece of paper. Beneath the question, he listed the delivery van driver, the neighbors, the officer who escorted Annie home, kids walking home from school, passersby. The bank robber if he'd been watching the place.

Curt's breath caught in his throat. He scribbled *Kai Aldred*, underlined it, and jabbed his pencil into the page.

The murder happened before they picked him up for squatting in Annie's house. And given the peepholes he'd drilled through the ceiling, he could've easily become fixated with her. He'd obviously built a rapport with Bella, given his daily comings and goings. And they only had Kai's word for it that he didn't hang around in the attic when Annie was at home. Since Bella had grown accustomed to Kai's presence in the house, she might not have alerted Annie if he had.

Or maybe Ray had discovered Kai in the house when he was installing the new locks and threatened to report him if he didn't clear out.

As much as the idea pained him, Curt had to consider that Kai might be Ray's killer.

The man he'd let loose. The man living under Grace's roof.

16

$\mathcal{F}$inding her next consultation room empty, Annie walked to the reception area. "Has my four 'o clock not shown yet?" She was sure she had a full schedule.

Debbie scanned her computer screen. "That was supposed to be Bernie Dyball. He called this morning and canceled."

Recalling her earlier suspicions of the man, Annie pressed a palm to her suddenly queasy gut. She'd meant to collect a sample of Bernie's prints for Curt, but the news about Adams had obliterated everything else from her mind. "Did Bernie give a reason for canceling?"

"Said he already feels better." Debbie winked. "You better watch it, or you'll work yourself out of a job with that magic touch of yours."

Annie feigned a smile, even as her suspicions escalated. She returned to her office, debating whether to share her suspicions with Curt without the benefit of prints. Maybe she could still get some. She donned latex gloves, then retrieved Bernie's file folder from the records cabinet behind the reception area. With any luck, there'd be a clear finger- or thumbprint on the paperwork he'd completed for his first visit. She took the folder to her office, then slid the intake sheet into a new folder to give to Curt.

Then again, letting Curt see a client's private information would constitute a violation of patient confidentiality. What if her actions got the clinic in trouble?

She opened the folder and studied the page. Perhaps she could conceal the written part and have him dust the edges. As she searched her desk for tape to secure a smaller masking page over the sensitive information, her phone rang.

"Hello?" Annie answered.

"I'm so glad I caught you," Sylvie's breathless voice came over the line. "The receptionist said you were done for the day."

"What's wrong? Is it Noah?"

"No, my friend's daughter. She's a dancer and is supposed to be dancing in a show at the Founder's Day event this weekend, but she's injured herself."

"Bring her in. I can see her right away."

Sylvie hesitated. "That could be a problem. You see my friend can't afford the treatment, so I was hoping you might see the girl outside of the office. I'd pay you on the side. That way my friend would be none the wiser."

Annie winced. "I'm not sure that's a good idea." Gayle wouldn't be pleased. Neither would their insurance company if something went wrong.

"Please," Sylvie pleaded.

Annie wavered. After last night, she was surprised Sylvie would want her anywhere near Noah, but she supposed he was busy playing soccer. Still, she'd never forgive herself if she brought trouble his way. "Actually, I don't have my car here today."

"You could walk. We're at the community center around the corner from the clinic."

"Okay." Annie nibbled her bottom lip, the panic she'd felt at the sound of the firecrackers earlier threatening to resurge. "I'll get there as soon as I can." She hung up and called Curt.

The call went to voice mail.

"Hey, it's me. I'm done for the day, and your sister has asked me to meet her at the community center to check on a friend's little girl.

I was wondering how long it would be before you get here. I could walk over." She hesitated. "Call me back."

While she waited for Curt to return her call, she finished prepping Bernie's intake page.

Ten minutes later, a text came through from Sylvie. *I thought you'd be here by now. My friend's getting antsy.*

Leaving now, Annie texted back, then sent a separate text to Curt to let him know where she'd be. At the reception desk, she told Debbie to let Ian know she'd left for the day.

"Will do."

Annie strode across the lobby but paused at the main exit. Should she have asked Ian if he could spare a few minutes to run her to the community center? She tightened her grip on her purse strap and inhaled a calming breath. The street was bustling with families coming and going from the community center. Her stalker wouldn't be foolish enough to try anything in public.

Annie scanned the area for anyone loitering about.

A group of children passed by on the sidewalk. In the parking lot, one of the clinic's regulars locked her car doors and hurried toward the entrance.

Annie smiled a greeting as she held the door open for the other woman. Then she set off toward the community center, posture erect, chin up, acting every inch the confident woman. She hoped.

At the sound of footfalls, she glanced over her shoulder and lengthened her stride.

An average-size guy behind her, in black jeans and a hoodie, quickened his pace.

Her heart pounding, she started to jog. The footfalls grew louder and faster. She crossed in front of the row of cars heading into the community center parking lot, then dashed for the door. As she yanked it open, tires squealed.

Hoodie Guy slapped the hood of a car that must have cut him off.

Focused on him through the community center's glass door, Annie fumbled for her phone.

"What's wrong?" Sylvie asked, making her jump.

"I'm not sure." Annie gripped the door handle and peered outside once more. "I thought someone was following me."

"Your stalker?" Sylvie's voice rose to a panicked pitch.

"I don't know." Annie pressed her palm to her head.

Watching Noah and the little girl sitting on a bench beside him, Sylvie lowered her voice. "Then he knows where you are. What if this guy's sneaking around the back of the building right now?"

Curt raced through the front doors of the community center. "Sylvie, I'm here. Where are you?" he shouted into his cell phone.

"To your left."

He jerked his attention in that direction and spotted his sister flagging him from an office door.

She hurried toward him. "Am I ever glad to see you. I wasn't thinking." She clutched his arm, her hand trembling. "I never should've begged Annie to come here."

"Is she hurt? Where's Noah?"

"In the main office. Follow me." She retraced her steps down the hall. "A guy in a black hoodie was following her, so the director let us use his office to wait for you. I was terrified the man would sneak in here and find her with us."

"Dad!" Noah shouted when Curt reached the door, and captured him in a bear hug.

Curt scanned the others in the room. "Is everyone all right?"

"I hurt my leg," a little girl said. "But Ms. Annie is helping it get better."

"She's good at that." Curt's gaze locked with Annie's over the child's head. "You okay?" he asked.

She smiled. "I'm good."

Since Annie was still treating the child's leg under her mother's anxious eye, Curt asked Noah to sit near his friend so he could speak to Sylvie. Curt drew Sylvie back into the hallway. "Is Annie sure the man was following her? He couldn't have simply been heading in the same direction, could he?" His sister had been keyed up ever since hearing Annie's stalker story.

"No. I saw him myself. Annie darted ahead of a line of cars, and when he tried to follow, a car cut him off. He was irate. He slapped the hood, and I think he swore at the driver."

"Did you know the driver?"

She started at the question, her brow furrowing. "No. What's that got to do with anything?"

"The driver might have gotten a better look at the guy. And I might be able to lift prints from his hood."

Sylvie frowned. "I never thought of that. I never paid attention to the car, except it was silver. I think. Maybe blue."

Great. That description covered the vast majority of the cars in the parking lot. But part of him itched to call in every available officer to canvass every driver in the place, because it was the closest he'd come to getting a description of Annie's saboteur. And it had to be him, because Curt had already questioned Kai, and Joey was presumed dead.

Curt momentarily debated using the PA system to ask the driver of the car to come forward. But half the parents didn't stick around while their kids were in class. Not to mention that if he publicly announced the police were seeking information, the driver could become a target too. "If we walk around the parking lot, do you think you'd recognize the car that cut off the culprit?"

"I doubt it."

The little girl and her mother exited the room. As they passed, the mom said, "We're all done. Thanks, Sylvie. Your friend really helped. I hope everything works out."

Noah raced to Curt. "Can Ms. Annie come for supper?"

Sylvie interjected, "Noah, I don't—"

"That's a great idea." Curt lifted his voice to override his sister's objection. "What do you say, Annie?"

Annie shifted her weight. "Given the situation, it's probably better if—"

"Let me stop you right there. There have been several new developments in your case since this morning. Trust me, joining us for dinner is a great idea." Curt ignored the tension radiating from Sylvie. Annie's situation was exactly why he preferred not to let her out of his sight.

"You're sure?"

"Yes."

Her lips trembled into a tentative smile. "We'll need to stop by my place to feed Bella and let her out for a bit."

"You can bring her to our place," Noah blurted. "Can't she, Dad?"

"Sure, she'd probably love the chance to visit someplace new."

Annie sucked in an exaggerated breath. "You have no idea what you're getting yourself into."

Curt chuckled at her feigned concern. "It'll be fine."

"We'd better get going, then," Sylvie said to Noah.

"Can't I go with you, Dad? I can keep Bella company in the back seat."

Curt glanced at Sylvie, who waved her hand dismissively. "Whatever."

Guilt gnawed at his gut that once again, she was being left out. "How about I pick up pizza for supper?"

"No need. I have chicken curry in the slow cooker."

"You're the best. Thanks."

By the time they arrived at the house with Bella in tow, Sylvie's mood had darkened considerably.

Annie suggested to Noah that they throw a ball outside with Bella for a few minutes. "Give her a chance to burn off all her pent-up energy before dinner."

Noah eagerly agreed and showed Annie to the backyard.

The moment the door closed behind them, Sylvie laid into Curt. "Having her here is a bad idea. What if her stalker sees her with Noah? He could use him to get to her."

"It's fine."

"It's not. Have you forgotten the rock-throwing incident? Not to mention Ray's murder."

Curt narrowed his eyes. "How'd you hear about that?"

She drew back. "Are you kidding me? You told me you found him dead, and county PD are investigating. The chief wouldn't bring them in if Ray died of natural causes."

Reluctantly, Curt acknowledged her argument.

"And Ray was working on Annie's place. What if her stalker saw him there? Or saw that hug she gave him in the middle of the church parking lot on Sunday? Things like that send psychos over the edge."

Annie came in the back door at the tail end of his sister's rant. "Excuse me. I didn't mean to interrupt, but can you tell me where the restroom is? I'd like to wash my hands before dinner."

"That way." Curt pointed down the hall. When Annie returned, he said to her and his sister, "I was planning to wait until after

Noah went to bed to tell you, but since I'm sure you overheard Sylvie's concerns, I'll tell you both now, while he's playing with Bella outside." He shifted closer to the window, so he could keep his eye on Noah. "County PD already have someone in custody for Adams's murder."

Annie's countenance brightened. "Wow, that was fast."

"Yes, the perpetrator left evidence that gave him away."

"And they think this is the guy who cut Annie's brakes too?" Sylvie asked.

"Since the murder investigation is ongoing and the county's domain, I'm afraid I can't say more than that."

Clearly irritated by his stonewalling, Sylvie snapped, "He can't be Annie's stalker. The guy followed Annie to the community center this afternoon."

"The guy you saw was *not* Joey Carmello." Curt strained to contain his annoyance with Sylvie's outbursts, even as he realized he'd probably respond the same way if he were in her shoes.

"How do you know it's not?" Sylvie spit, her fear changing her into someone he scarcely recognized.

"Because Joey was killed six years ago."

Annie gasped, her eyes rounding. "He was?"

"Yes. I found out this morning." But what if his compulsion to protect Annie had made him want to accept the story as fact too easily, and overridden his good sense when it came to safeguarding Noah?

As if a crushing weight had been lifted from her shoulders, Annie stood taller. The worry lines around her eyes and mouth faded. Her expression shone with renewed joy.

Curt shook his doubts aside. "As I said from the beginning, it appears the attacks against you were the frantic attempts of our bank robber to scare you off."

A little of the light drained from Annie's eyes. "Then who sent the flowers?"

Curt grimaced. Kai had steadfastly denied sending the flowers to Annie. Then again, he'd denied murdering Adams too. But the fact he had no transportation to get him to a shop twenty minutes outside of town made it more probable he was telling the truth about the flowers.

Curt held Annie's gaze. "Because of everything that's happened, we've tended to assume the worst about every incident. But the card accompanying the flowers could have been as innocuous as it sounded. Anyone from a neighbor to a client might've written it after hearing of your troubles."

Annie pressed her lips together, tears pooling in her eyes. "How awful that someone went to all that trouble to brighten my day and I twisted it into something horrible."

Curt made a mental note to ask his friend to dig deeper into Joey's disappearance. On the off chance the story was fabricated, Curt needed to know if Joey could still be alive somewhere, but he didn't want to risk his search for information being linked to Safe Haven.

Thankfully, Sylvie let the subject drop and busied herself dishing up supper.

Annie asked how she could help, but Sylvie shooed her outside to fetch Noah while Curt set the table.

"I'm sorry I got testy," he said to his sister. "I hope you know how much I appreciate all you do for us."

Sylvie shot him a wry smile. "There's no place I'd rather be. You know that. But I guess I sounded as grumpy as a mama bear fending for her cub."

"And I love that you care about Noah that much."

Her expression softened. "I do. I don't know what I'd do without him."

Supper and the rest of the evening passed amiably, until Sylvie announced that it was Noah's bedtime.

"Ms. Annie, can you read me my bedtime story?" Noah pleaded.

"I'd love to," Annie said, allowing him to lead her to his room.

The moment they disappeared through the doorway, Sylvie grew sullen. "I guess I might as well be off." She tugged on her coat, clearly not pleased that her usual routine with Noah had been usurped.

Curt rose and gave her a hug. "Thanks again for a delicious meal."

She rolled her eyes. "Call me when you're ready to drive Annie home and I'll come back and sit with Noah."

"That won't be necessary."

Sylvie's countenance turned stormy. "You're not intending to let her stay here."

"No. I've arranged for a female officer to stay with Annie."

Sylvie acknowledged the arrangement with a brisk nod.

After locking the door behind his sister, Curt wandered down the hall to look in on Annie and Noah. Bella was snuggled up to Noah on one side, with Annie on the other. She was reading his favorite bedtime story, complete with different voices for each character. Every so often, Noah interjected a snippet of dialogue he remembered by heart, while attempting to deepen his voice to sound more like the character. The tender scene stirred a longing deep in Curt's soul, and his breath hitched.

He'd been sure such feelings had died with Beth. That he was destined to live the rest of his life on his own, a single parent. It was safer that way. Safer for Noah and for his own heart. From the moment his wife died, he'd done everything possible to protect Noah from harm. He'd even questioned the wisdom of allowing his boy to play competitive soccer. Yet for all his extra caution, he hadn't been able to resist the compulsion to protect Annie, not even in the face of Sylvie's fears.

His son felt the pull too. Annie's selfless caring and upbeat outlook, despite her own troubles, drew them like an irresistible magnet. In anyone else, her stubborn streak might have driven him mad, but crossing wits with her challenged him in an oddly exhilarating way.

The story ended, and Noah begged for another.

"Not tonight," Curt said from the doorway. "It's already late, and you have school in the morning."

"Okay." He gave Annie a spontaneous hug. "Can Bella stay with me until you go home?"

"If it's all right with your dad." Annie climbed off the bed and tucked the covers around him.

"Can she, Dad?" Noah asked.

"As long as you actually go to sleep," Curt told him. He exchanged places with Annie to say a prayer with his son.

Noah squeezed his eyes shut and clasped his hands. "Lord, thank you that Annie and Bella could visit tonight. Please help Jenny's leg feel better fast. Bless Aunt Sylvie and Grandma Grace and Dad and Annie. And please help Dad catch the bad guy who's trying to hurt her."

"Amen." Curt peeked at Annie, who was standing in the doorway.

She'd also closed her eyes and bowed her head. Inhaling, she pressed her lips together and lifted her shoulders as if savoring a cosmic assurance that his son's prayers were heard.

Curt kissed Noah and patted Bella before joining Annie outside the bedroom door.

When he stopped beside her, she lifted her face, and her misty blue eyes met his, her expression serene. He caressed her cheek with his thumb, and his senses ignited. Her delicate vanilla scent encircled them. Her eyes beamed admiration, gratitude, and something else he hesitated to define but that reached inside and squeezed his heart.

His gaze dropped to her mouth, and before he'd registered his intention, he inclined his head and pressed his lips to hers.

She didn't pull away.

He cradled her face in his hands, then curled his fingers beneath her hair. She tasted of peach tea and sunshine and—and impossible dreams. He abruptly drew back.

Her eyelashes fluttered open. At the sight of her shy, somewhat dazed expression, he stroked her cheek once more, unwilling to pull away entirely.

The magnitude of the mistake he'd just made weighed heavily on his chest. He couldn't afford to be so distracted. How could he keep her safe if he were so easily taken off his guard? "I—"

"Don't you dare apologize," she interrupted.

He smiled. To deny that it had been phenomenal would be a crime. "I was going to say, I'm afraid that wasn't very professional of me."

She smiled. "Being professional is sometimes overrated."

Not if it's the only way I'll be able to keep you safe.

Being professional is overrated. Where had that come from? She sounded like a lovesick teenager. Ducking her head, Annie led the way to Curt's living room. She couldn't deny how safe she felt around him, despite all the scary things happening to her. If anything, it was a little scary how natural it had become to lean on him in such a short amount of time.

And then there was Noah. Her heart had soared when the boy hugged her good night.

If she was honest with herself, she'd been wondering what it might be like to kiss Curt. She flattened her palm against the flutter in her chest. *Is this how it feels to truly care for someone?*

His scent wrapped her in warmth and comfort, as she perched on the end of his sofa and sipped her water. People often remarked on how caring she was, but she felt like a fraud when they did, because she'd trained herself to ask questions to draw others out and refrain from talking about herself out of self-preservation. It was nothing more than a habit—a habit that served her well in her profession. But she'd become so adept at projecting interest in her patients' concerns, while maintaining a safe emotional distance, that she wasn't sure she was capable of genuinely caring for anyone.

Curt sank into the armchair opposite her. "We need to talk about your safety."

She blinked and set down her glass. *Safety? But Joey's dead.* She'd never felt such relief as when Curt had said it. She could finally, *finally* stop running.

He took her hand, and the sweeping caress of his thumb across the back of her wrist muddled her thoughts even more. "Although Kai is in custody for Ray's murder, and Carmello is out of the picture, the—"

"Wait. *Kai* killed Ray? Why?" She couldn't imagine the young man being capable of such a violent act.

A pained expression flitted across Curt's features. "I'm not at liberty to discuss the evidence."

She frowned. "Did Ray catch him at my house and threaten to turn him in if he didn't move out?"

"That's one theory." Curt steepled his fingers in his lap and she immediately missed the warmth of his touch. "We don't know his motive. He's not talking."

"Please tell me he didn't fixate on me like Joey did." She shivered at the memory of the peepholes in her ceiling.

Curt's jaw muscle twitched. "I admit it crossed my mind. I thought he might have sent you the flowers, but they were ordered in person at a shop twenty minutes north of town. Kai doesn't have a vehicle, so it's unlikely. However, County PD will probably question the cashier to rule out the possibility."

Annie sobered. "You wanted me to believe a patient or neighbor sent the flowers."

"That does seem most likely. The cashier mentioned that a silver-haired gentleman had placed an order, as well as a young mother and her son."

"The silver-haired guy could have been who Kai saw in my backyard. Didn't Kai have the impression it was an older guy?"

"Kai described the person from your backyard as 'stooped over,' but that could be because that person was fiddling with the exhaust pipe. I doubt the guy would go from making two attempts on your life to sending you flowers. Unless—" Something flashed in Curt's eyes.

"Unless what?"

"Unless he chose a ready-made bouquet for delivery and inserted a listening device into it. I'll have to take a closer look at that possibility."

Annie shuddered at the idea the creep could have been listening to her. She was always talking, whether telling Bella her plans or giving herself a pep talk.

"Either way," Curt continued, "the appearance of that guy in the hoodie this afternoon means we can't assume our bank robber has decided to leave you alone."

"So I'm no safer than before?" She hated how her voice cracked, but the notion that the creep had planted a listening device in the bouquet made her wish Curt would install her in a safe house. She certainly wouldn't be using her furnace anytime soon.

"To be honest, I'd prefer to keep you here in my guest room, where I could watch out for you." Curt's eyes locked on hers, and her heart did the little jig it did whenever he was around.

She felt safe with him, but she had to refuse. "That could endanger Noah." Sylvie was right. She shouldn't have gone to Curt's house at all. "I won't risk anything happening to your son."

"I agree it's too big a risk. So I asked one of our female officers, Bev Young, to bunk with you. That way you'll still have trained eyes watching out for you. Are you okay with that?"

She hesitated. Having a stranger sleep in her guest room would feel a little weird.

"It's either that or I park outside your house all night."

Annie pursed her lips. "You wouldn't."

"I would."

"Fine. Officer Young can stay with me."

"Good." Curt scrolled through his contact list and tapped a name. "I was going to have her pick you up here, but I think I'll ask Sylvie to come back and stay with Noah for half an hour, so I can sweep your place for listening devices."

"What's up?" Sylvie's voice issued from Curt's phone, muffled by what sounded like wind.

Curt rose and, pushing aside the drapes, glanced toward his sister's place. "Are you out?"

"For a walk, yeah. Needed to clear my head. Why?"

"I was hoping you could stay with Noah for a bit."

The silence that followed made Annie wish she hadn't agreed to the change in plans. The other officer could have swept her place for bugs. They'd already raised Sylvie's ire enough for one day. The last thing she needed was another reminder of the potential danger to her beloved nephew.

"Sylvie?" Curt prompted.

"Yes. Of course I can." She sounded breathless, as if maybe she'd started jogging. "Give me fifteen minutes."

"You're the best. Thanks." While Curt waited for his sister to return, he called Officer Young and asked her to meet them at Annie's house in half an hour.

Twenty minutes later, Curt parked at the end of her driveway.

When they'd picked Bella up earlier, Annie had left several lights on inside the house, as well as the porch light. Sheers covered the front windows, making it impossible to see anything but shadows. But she couldn't see anything moving about inside or lurking in the porch area.

Curt stayed her hand when she reached behind the seat for Bella's leash. "Before we go in, I'd like you to wait in the car while I check the perimeter."

"All right," Annie said, even though she was pretty sure he wasn't actually offering a choice.

When Curt hit the locks with his key fob, Bella whined.

"He won't be long." Annie clutched her phone as Curt disappeared behind the garage.

A loud *whomp* shook the passenger window.

Annie screamed, her gaze snapping to the window. "Colin Mitchell." She jabbed the window button to no avail, since Curt had shut off the car.

Barking, Bella slapped her paws at the glass closest to Colin, who stood straddling his bicycle next to the car.

"Got ya, Ms. Bishop." He gave her a smug grin. "What are you doing sitting out here?"

Annie flicked off the lock and shoved open the door. "Ensuring that troublemakers like you aren't lurking about."

"Police. Hands in the air," Curt ordered, his weapon trained on Colin's back.

Colin's hands shot up.

It was Annie's turn to grin. "And that's my bodyguard."

Curt ordered Colin to the ground.

"Tell him I didn't do anything," Colin whispered to her.

"Keep your hands up," Curt shouted.

Annie surged to her feet before things escalated. "It's okay, Curt. Colin was riding home and wondered why I was sitting in my driveway."

Curt's eyes narrowed, though he holstered the gun. "You screamed."

"He surprised me." To Colin, she added, "Officer Porter told you your pranks were going to get you into trouble."

Despite her teasing, Colin's body remained tense. "Can I put my hands down now?"

"Fine," Curt said. "Go on."

Colin didn't need any more encouragement. Without so much as a glance in Curt's direction, he took off on his bike.

Annie apologized for the excitement and let Bella out of the back seat. "Is it safe to go in now?"

"Yes."

Once inside, Annie rearmed the security system for stay mode. Then she reviewed the surveillance footage of the last few hours at triple speed while Curt repeated his check for intruders and swept the place for bugs.

Suddenly, Annie paused the footage with a sharp intake of breath, rewinding it to a grainy image of someone in a hoodie approaching the garage.

Curt returned in time to see her staring. He squinted at the image, then advanced the feed. "He never looks toward the camera."

"And seems to change his mind about approaching the house." Annie's heart pounded painfully. "Why?"

"The motion sensor lights could've spooked him. Or maybe someone came by on the street." Curt stopped the feed. "I think he left something in the bushes. Wait here."

Curt snapped on a pair of latex gloves, then momentarily disabled the alarm and slipped out into the night. Two minutes later, he knocked on the door.

Annie let him back inside. "What is it?"

Curt's jaw muscle tensed. "A photograph." He slid it into an evidence bag before letting her see it.

Her blood went cold at the sight of her own image in the candid photo—her eyes scratched out. "That was taken at the orchard when I was with you and Noah."

Curt gave an anguished, guttural sound.

"He was watching us." Annie's breath stalled in her throat. "He saw me with Noah."

Curt downed his second cup of coffee the next morning. He'd scarcely slept for worrying about Annie and his son. But at least Officer Young's morning report had taken the edge off his frayed nerves. There'd been no more incidents at Annie's place since last night. "Noah, are you ready? The bus will be here before you know it," Curt called down the hall as he snagged his ringing cell phone. "Porter here."

"Hey, it's Dan."

Curt checked his watch. They still had forty-five minutes before their shift began. "You're at the station already? What's up?"

"I thought you'd want to know that Kai Aldred was released yesterday."

"Why?"

"He has a rock-solid alibi. He worked a double shift Monday. And video surveillance proves he was there the entire time. He couldn't have killed Adams."

Picturing the grainy image on Annie's surveillance video, Curt felt his jaw tighten. Could their hoodie-wearing photographer have been Kai? "I can't believe they didn't notify me. They know I consider him a potential threat to An—Ms. Bishop."

"I guess they figured this negated your concerns in that department too."

Grateful Dan couldn't see his grimace, Curt thanked his colleague for the heads-up. "I'll hit Ms. Bishop's place before coming in."

"Roger that."

Curt holstered his gun, kissed Noah goodbye, and asked Sylvie to make sure he got on the bus. Halfway to his car, he doubled back and said, "On second thought, it might be better if you drive him to school today. Do you mind?"

The concern she flashed him told him she knew exactly why he was asking. "I don't mind at all," she said without so much as an

I-told-you-so. She'd wait until Noah wasn't around to give him the lecture he probably deserved.

Backing out of the driveway, Curt said to his phone, "Call Bev Young."

The officer staying with Annie picked up on the second ring.

"Everything still okay there?" he asked.

"Um."

He didn't like the sound of that. "What's wrong?"

"Annie went out."

"What do you mean, out? You're supposed to be guarding her."

"She left a note when I was in the shower. Said the dog was getting stir-crazy and she took it for a quick spin around the block."

Curt floored the gas. "You head east down the street and look for her. I'm coming in from the west."

"On it."

Seething, he hung up. How could Annie be so careless? Bella was not a guard dog, especially against the likes of Kai Aldred, who'd been coming and going from the house at will for weeks.

Curt was three blocks from her house in record time. He slammed on his brakes at the intersection as a group of kids started across the street. Scanning the street in both directions, Curt spotted Annie a block away, rounding the corner at a carefree lope, and he took his first full breath since talking to Officer Young.

Then Kai Aldred burst from the next side street, eyes wild.

Curt honked at the schoolchildren dawdling in the crosswalk in front of him. When Kai dashed toward Annie, Curt swerved around the kids.

Annie yanked Bella away from Kai, then froze at the squeal of Curt's tires.

Shouting, Kai grabbed her arm.

18

$\mathcal{C}$urt careened to a stop at Annie's side as she struggled to twist free of Kai's grip.

Bella went into a barking frenzy.

Drawing his weapon, Curt sprang out from behind the wheel. Using his vehicle as cover, he took a bead on Kai. "Let her go, Kai."

Kai's hands instantly shot up, his face crimson from his frantic sprint. "I wasn't going to hurt her. I came to warn her." He gestured to Annie. "He's at Grace's. The geezer who tried to kill you." Kai's panicked gaze shot back to Curt. "You have to get him. He's at Grace's."

"Who's at Grace's?" Annie asked.

Kai plowed his fingers through his hair. "The guy in the hoodie. I was coming home from my shift and saw him go in the side door. So I snuck up and peeked in the window."

"And what was he doing?"

"Drinking coffee at the kitchen table with Grace." Kai winced. "You don't think he'll hurt her too, do you?" A horrified expression twisted Kai's features. "I shouldn't have left her."

Officer Young dashed toward them.

Curt motioned to Kai. "Take him to the station to get a full statement. We'll need him to provide an ID when I bring in the suspect." He opened the passenger door for Annie.

Annie squeezed Kai's shoulder. "You did the right thing. Thank you, Kai."

Bella wriggled into the vehicle at Annie's feet, and Curt eased the door closed.

"I think I know who Kai saw," Annie said, the instant Curt slid behind the steering wheel. "Grace's friend Bernie. He had coffee with her Saturday morning too. And he was my last client Friday afternoon, before you noticed the brake fluid under my car."

"Why didn't you tell me this before?"

She flinched. "I didn't think of him until I heard Kai's description of the stooped man he saw in my yard, but I didn't want to accuse Grace's friend without proof."

"We're hunting a potential murderer. Grace would have understood."

Annie twisted her fingers in Bella's leash. "I'd planned to bring you something with his fingerprints so you could compare them to the others. But with yesterday's excitement, I forgot all about it."

Whining, Bella laid her head in Annie's lap, and Annie scratched her neck. "There's something else I haven't thought to tell you."

Curt slowed the car, wanting to hear Annie out before he confronted the guy. "Go on."

"At Bernie's appointment, I drew his attention to an old scar and he reacted oddly. The scar resembled a bullet wound and I thought maybe he'd served in the military. But the scar made me think of Joey too, so I might've acted weird myself." She sucked in a breath. "Maybe Bernie misinterpreted my reaction as my recognizing him from the bank robbery."

Tamping down his frustration that it was the first time he was hearing about a potentially dangerous suspect, Curt pulled into Grace's driveway and parked behind another vehicle. "Stay here."

"His car's gone," Annie blurted. "Bernie drives a different car. That's Ian's."

Grace ambled out onto the porch, followed by Gayle and Ian.

"Hello, you two. Is everything okay?"

Annie climbed out of the passenger seat. Curt shot her a scowl as she asked, "Did your friend Bernie come for coffee this morning?"

"Why, yes. How did you know?" Grace responded.

Hesitating, Annie chewed on her bottom lip and deferred the explanation to Curt.

"Did anyone else stop by for coffee this morning?" Curt asked.

"No," Grace answered.

Her son stepped forward, his gaze shifting from Annie to Curt. "What's going on?"

"Kai Aldred claims your mom's friend is the person he saw in Annie's backyard on Friday."

"Tampering with the furnace pipe?" Grace asked. "Why would Bernie hurt Annie?"

"Do you still have the coffee mug he used? Or anything else he touched?"

"Yes, I must. I didn't have a chance to clean up yet because Gayle and Ian stopped by with vegetables from their garden for me."

Curt snapped on a pair of latex gloves. "Could you show me which mug he used?" A moment later, he rejoined Annie and the Kemps on the front porch. "I'll get this dusted for prints. If they're a match, I should be able to secure an arrest warrant before noon."

Grace covered her mouth with a trembling hand. "I can't believe Bernie would do such a thing."

Ian circled an arm around his mother's shoulders. "You couldn't know. Do you think Mom's in any danger, Officer?"

Curt scanned the street. "Not once I have Bernie in custody." He opened the door for Annie to climb back into his car. "I'll have Officer Young bring you home or to work once we've got him." In case Bernie had spotted Kai peering through Grace's kitchen window.

"I have appointments starting at ten," Annie protested.

Curt glanced at his dashboard clock. "We'll get you there in time." Driving to the station, he phoned in a BOLO request for Bernie's car and for officers to check the man's house.

Kai, waiting in a conference room at the station, became antsier than ever when they walked in without their suspect.

Curt left Officer Young with Annie, Bella, and Kai while he ran Bernie's prints.

Twenty minutes later, shouting drew him out into the hall.

"There he is." Kai pointed to a small-framed person in a dark blue hoodie in the lobby.

The person turned.

"Gayle?" Annie blurted. "Gayle was the person you saw at Grace's?"

"Well, no," Kai explained, "but the guy had the same twirly logo on the back of his hoodie."

"But he was a guy?"

"I don't know. I saw him from behind." Kai jabbed his finger at her shirt. "But that's the shirt all right."

Oblivious to the allegation, Gayle and Ian hurried toward them. "We thought you might need a ride to work."

Curt ushered them all into the conference room. "Did you two see Bernie at your mother's this morning?"

"Sure, he was finishing his coffee when we arrived," Gayle said.

"Was he wearing a hoodie like yours?"

Gayle frowned at her hooded sweatshirt. "I—I don't recall."

"He wore a brown leather jacket," Ian interjected.

Curt deflated. Kai had led them on a wild goose chase. *Was it on purpose?*

A technician rapped on the door, then poked his head around the frame and held up a sheet of paper. "You've got your match."

Stunned, Curt stared at him for a full five seconds before he found his voice. "The prints on the mug match the ones from the brake line and the furnace pipe?" Curt clarified.

"Not the ones on the pipe. The one from the brake line. You want me to start the paperwork for an arrest warrant?"

"Yeah." Curt shifted his attention to Gayle. "Did you touch any mugs at Grace's this morning?"

Annie gasped at his implication.

Gayle chuckled. "No. I always carry my own brew in the mornings in my thermal mug."

"Then the two of you can see Annie to work, because I have a bad guy to catch."

"Would that be all right?"

Annie snapped out of her daydreaming at her elderly client's question. "I'm sorry. What did you ask?"

The woman repeated her inquiry, and Annie clarified her earlier instructions, then held the consulting room's door open for the patient to exit. Glancing at her watch, she stepped into her office before attending to her next client. She grabbed a water bottle and checked her cell phone for messages.

Still no word from Curt.

Annie paced the room. She should feel more at ease. After all, Joey was dead. And thanks to the fingerprint match, despite Kai's mistaken ID, Curt would soon have Bernie in custody—if he didn't already. She'd be able to start enjoying her new life in Safe Haven without having to peer over her shoulder. Maybe she'd even spend more time with Curt and Noah—as a person, rather than as a victim to protect.

Maybe even as something more. The possibility whispered to her heart. She'd left behind any hope of a happily-ever-after with her old life in Chicago. But Curt and Noah had rekindled dreams she'd previously been determined to relinquish.

Her mind's eye flicked to Sylvie's irritation over her being at Curt's house last night. Annie couldn't blame his sister. Maybe Bernie's arrest would mollify her.

After gulping another swig of water, Annie left her bottle and phone on her desk and returned to the consultation room to greet her next client.

She repeated the pattern for the next two hours. But still no word came from Curt.

What if Bernie skipped town before Curt could get to him?

Annie shored up her flagging spirits with a deep breath and opened her office door.

The receptionist stood outside, a gorgeous floral arrangement in one hand, her other poised to knock on Annie's door. "These arrived for you. I ran to the bathroom and they were there on the desk when I got back."

Annie's eyes widened. Was it how Curt had decided to share the good news? She took the vase from Debbie—then registered the sunflowers dominating the bouquet. At the thought of the last flowers she'd received, a cold sweat coated her skin.

As if Debbie could read her thoughts, she murmured, "Ian checked these over and said to assure you they're safe."

Relaxing a fraction, Annie retreated into her office and set the arrangement on her desk. With trembling fingers, she retrieved a small envelope clipped to a plastic holder spiked among the flowers. When she saw that it was still sealed, her heart thumped. Had Ian opted not to open it because he knew the delivery came from Curt?

She slit the top of the envelope with her letter opener and removed the card. The front simply said: *For Annie.* No signature. She flipped it over and stifled a cry.

I'm not dead. But next time, someone you love might be. JC.

19

*H*is siren blaring, Curt headed for a gas station outside of town where Bernie's car had been spotted. His cell phone rang, and he answered over the hands-free system. "I can't talk now, Annie. I'm trying to catch Bernie."

"Joey's not dead. He's here."

Curt's breath stalled in his throat. "At the clinic?"

"No, but he's in Safe Haven. He sent more flowers." She gulped audibly. "He signed them this time."

Curt tightened his grip on the steering wheel. The card could be a hoax. Or had someone in Chicago PD manufactured the intel given to his friend that Joey Carmello was presumed dead?

Annie read him the card, and Curt bit his lip. The note found under Ray's body had sounded like something Joey would write too. And Kai had alibied out of the murder. Maybe it wasn't a hoax.

A pedestrian bobbing to the music playing in his ears stepped onto the street.

Curt laid on his horn and skirted the jaywalker. "Bernie's fingerprints were a match," he protested, trying to mask the fear and exasperation but failing. "The flowers have to be a smoke screen." One he couldn't deal with at the moment. Not if he was going to nab Bernie before the man disappeared. "Bernie is your saboteur, Annie. Grace probably mentioned something to him about your stalker, giving him the idea to play on your fears with that card."

"I never told Grace about my stalker, but even if Gayle and Ian did, I never told them Joey's name. And the card is signed JC."

Curt's heart ricocheted off his ribs. "Stay at the clinic until I can get there. And let me talk to Ian." If Joey wanted to terrorize Annie, why have the Chicago PD seed false information about his supposed demise? Curt squared his jaw at the probable answer: so any cop investigating her claims would dismiss them as fear-induced rants.

"What do you need me to do?" Ian's voice reached into Curt's car.

"Keep Annie safe. All our personnel are closing in on Bernie. We don't have anyone else to send there right now."

"No problem. You focus on bringing in the perp. We'll make sure no one gets in here who shouldn't. We've already locked down the clinic and will only admit scheduled patients."

"Good work. I've got to go." Curt hung up and focused on the line of police vehicles hemming in Bernie's car.

"You've got nowhere to go, Dyball," a sergeant from the county PD declared through his bullhorn. "Lay down your weapon."

Shielded by their vehicles, officers aimed their guns at the elderly man. A sniper moved into position on the roof of a nearby building.

"I'm not going to jail," Dyball shouted. "I knew she could ID me."

Curt's gut solidified into a hard rock. If the situation went down as he suspected it might, Bernie could die without Curt getting the chance to ask him if he'd sent Annie the flowers. Curt approached the commander on scene and asked for the bullhorn so he could speak to Bernie. "Annie can't ID you for that old robbery."

Bernie's attention snapped toward Curt.

"All we've got you for is tampering with her brakes," Curt continued. "Lay down your weapon and turn yourself in. Things will go easier for you that way."

"That's what they told my dad, and he died in jail," Bernie bellowed.

"Why'd you do it, Bernie?" Curt asked. "The statute of limitations on the bank job was up. We couldn't have charged you, even if Annie could ID you."

The wrinkles in the man's forehead deepened. "I—" He tightened his grip on the gun. "You're trying to confuse me."

"We lifted your prints from Annie's brake line. They match the ones left by the armed robber in that old case."

Bernie readjusted his hold on the weapon but didn't reply.

Curt moved the bullhorn away from his mouth to speak to the sergeant. "Tell your sniper to stand down. This guy could be my link to a possible second suspect. I need him alive."

"Hold your fire," the sergeant said into his radio.

Curt squinted at Dyball. "You were smart to leave the note under Ray's body," he said, fishing. "You didn't leave any prints on that one."

Bernie frowned. "I don't know what you're talking about."

"You know, the note to Annie. Like the one you sent her with the flowers today."

"I didn't send any flowers."

Curt's gut clenched. Bernie could be lying. He had to know that admitting to sending the flowers and therefore the accompanying note was tantamount to confessing to Ray's murder.

Bernie swiped the back of his sleeve across his upper lip. "I wasn't in my right mind Friday. She saw my scar and I panicked. I'm not that guy anymore."

"Did you think Ray could ID you too?" Curt asked.

"What? I don't know anyone named Ray." Bernie waved his gun at Curt. "You're trying to confuse me again."

Curt kept his voice gentle. "I'm trying to get to the truth, because if you didn't do the other things, there's still someone out there trying to hurt Annie. You said you're not a bad guy anymore, so prove that. Help me find him, and I can help you in return."

As if he'd been tossed a lifeline, hope sparked in the man's face. "Help me stay out of jail?"

"Maybe." Given the man's references to confusion, Curt was pretty sure a good lawyer could get Bernie into a mental health facility on a diminished-capacity defense.

"I haven't done anything to her since Friday."

Curt cringed. Had his fishing call to Chicago PD triggered everything else? Except he hadn't made the call until around the time of the rock-throwing incident. Could that have been kids, as the deputy speculated? "So, you admit to cutting Ms. Bishop's brakes?"

Bernie's head wobbled from side to side.

"Did you throw rocks at her? Lure her to a dead-end street? Light firecrackers as she was coming out of her workplace?"

Bernie's brows slashed downward.

"If you want my help, I need the truth," Curt prodded.

"I—" The gun fell from Bernie's hand, and he clutched his chest.

"Bernie?" Curt rushed forward and, kicking the gun out of the man's reach, eased him to the ground.

Whatever Bernie had been about to say came out as an agonized groan.

"Stay with me," Curt pleaded, then yelled over his shoulder. "I need a paramedic over here." Curt loosened Bernie's collar. "I need to know if you sent Annie the flowers. The truth. Come on, Bernie."

The older man's gaze fixed on Curt's, but then his eyes slid shut and his body went limp.

As the paramedics nudged Curt out of their way, the knot in his gut rammed into his throat. Bernie had tampered with Annie's brakes. Chances were that he was good for the rest.

But until Curt was certain, he couldn't ignore that there might be someone else out there who was intent on terrorizing her.

During a lull between patients, Annie paced her office. *I never should've come to Safe Haven. How did Joey find me?*

She grabbed the wastepaper basket holding the flowers she'd dumped and tromped down the hallway toward the back door.

"What are you doing?" Ian asked from behind her.

Startled, she fumbled the basket, spilling the contents. "Throwing these out." She crammed the wretched flowers back inside. "I can't stand the sight of them any longer."

His expression became sympathetic. "Let me do that." He picked up the last of the blooms and relieved her of the wastebasket. "You okay?"

She wrapped her arms around her midriff. "Not really, no."

"Hopefully, by the time Curt gets back, your troubles will be over."

Annie forced herself to acknowledge the wishful thinking with a nod, even though she knew it was a pipe dream. Arresting Bernie wouldn't stop Joey.

As if he'd read her thoughts, Ian told her not to worry. "The doors are locked. No one else is walking in here, unless we let them."

Today, maybe. But for how long after that? The fact that someone had come in unnoticed and left the bouquet on the reception desk had sent alarm bells clanging in Annie's head, and the uneventful hours since hadn't made the sound any less deafening. If Joey delivered the flowers himself, he could have walked straight into her office to wait for his chance to pounce.

Shaking the image from her mind, Annie returned to her office. A few minutes later, Curt knocked on her door. The warmth in his eyes eased the tension gripping her. He closed the distance between them and folded her into his arms. "We got him."

She accepted the comfort he offered, even as her mind screamed that she shouldn't. But Curt's gentle touch made her stomach flutter in a much more pleasant way than the churning it had been doing all day. She'd drawn on every ounce of inner fortitude to hide her anxiety from her clients. She wrapped her arms around his waist, her breath hitching on a dry sob. "But it's not over. Joey's still out there."

Curt eased his hold and searched her eyes. "Ian secured the card for me that came with your flowers. It was wiped clean. If Joey wanted to convince you he was alive, why would he do that?"

"Habit?" Exhaustion oozed from her voice. She didn't know how much longer she could endure the torment. "No one else makes sense. Or knows my history with Joey."

"Bernie might. He's a thief from Chicago, so he could've known Joey."

Hope flickered in her chest. "Did you ask him if he sent the bouquet?"

Curt's wince extinguished the spark. "I'm afraid he had a heart attack during his apprehension. His interrogation will have to wait."

"And what do we do in the meantime? Ignore the possibility that Joey is still out there?" Annie squeezed her hands into fists. "And he has to be, because even if Bernie knew about my connection to him, he would've known me as Kristie the ER nurse, not as Annie the physical therapist. Whoever your friend talked to at Chicago PD must have fed him a pack of lies. I haven't told anyone about Joey since I left that town."

"Not even Gayle and Ian?"

For some reason Curt's dogged resistance to the idea of Joey still being alive riled Annie to the point of wanting to scream. "After freaking out about my photo being on the clinic's website Monday, I told them I had a stalker. But I didn't tell them his name. I've never breathed Joey's name to anyone. Not until I told—"

Annie's breath stalled in her chest.

Because besides Curt, she'd only ever told one other person about Joey.

"Sylvie."

My sister? Curt stared at Annie, too stunned to respond. Sylvie wouldn't do such a horrible thing. She'd seen how terrorized her college roommate had been by a stalker. She'd never inflict that kind of torture on another woman. But even as his heart rebelled at the supposition, links dropped into place in his mind with unnerving clarity.

The last card addressed to Annie had said, "I'm not dead." And, besides Annie, Sylvie was the sole person with whom he had shared the information that Joey was dead.

Another realization sucked the air from his chest. The rock-throwing incident had happened the same afternoon Sylvie had claimed to be at an out-of-town craft show.

Had she even gone to the event? Or had she followed Annie to Pikes Peak, then pretended she'd arrived at the park at the same time he had. He spun away and paced Annie's office. "I can't believe Sylvie would do this."

"I think she made the call about Bella being missing too," Annie interjected. "She disguised her voice, but there was something familiar about the way she talked, and I've just realized what it was."

He snapped his attention back to Annie. "What's that?"

"The caller said, 'I need to be off.' I've heard Sylvie use a similar expression after Noah's appointments and other times."

Curt groaned, recognizing it as a phrase Sylvie often used. "I knew she was irritated that Noah kept asking to have you over, but she said it was because she was concerned about his safety." He scrubbed a hand over his face. "And it was all lies."

Annie shuddered. "Not *all* lies."

Curt scowled. "How do you figure?"

"None of this started until after Bernie tampered with my brakes. She had good reason to be concerned about Noah being seen anywhere near me."

Suddenly, Curt felt physically sick. His sister had always been the fearless one in the family. She'd go skydiving and bungee jumping and rock climbing without a second thought—until her college roommate's stalker. And Curt's all-consuming preoccupation with Noah's safety would have fed Sylvie's paranoia.

Annie sighed. "But yes, I suspect Noah's fondness for me bothers her too."

Curt closed his eyes for a moment before opening them again. "I could see she was hurt at Pikes Peak when Noah didn't want to go home with her. She'd already been annoyed with me for responding to the call, since it wasn't my jurisdiction. That probably convinced her that something more than duty compelled me."

Annie tilted her head. "Really?" A tiny smile hitched up a corner of her lips.

He grazed his knuckles across her cheek, desperate to find out whether she felt the connection too. "From the moment we met, I've felt drawn to you." He reclaimed her hand. "I don't know how else to explain it. I couldn't *not* protect you. Sylvie must've sensed as much." Curt growled in frustration. "When I moved here with Noah after my wife's death, Sylvie threw herself into the mothering role, and I was beyond grateful. Our parents died in a plane crash long before Noah came along, and my wife had no family left. Sylvie was all the family Noah and I had."

Annie squeezed his hand. "And you're all the family Sylvie has."

Curt groaned. "How did I not recognize how threatened she must have felt by Noah's growing attachment to you?"

Because she'd masked it as concern for Noah's safety.

He resumed his pacing.

Annie's face contorted in anguish. "I would never come between Noah and his aunt."

Another link streaked through Curt's mind. The flower shop clerk had mentioned that a mother and son had been among the customers she'd served Sunday. Could that have been Sylvie and Noah?

"What is it?" Annie asked after he didn't respond.

"I need to make a call." Curt searched his call history for the clerk's contact information. "I might have a way to verify whether Sylvie sent you the first bouquet."

The clerk answered, and Curt explained why he was calling.

"Sure. Message their photo to this number, and I'll tell you if I recognize them," she agreed.

Curt hung up, then scrolled through the photos on his phone. Finding a recent close-up of Sylvie and Noah together, he sent it to the clerk's phone. "Now we wait." He clenched and unclenched his hand, still not wanting to believe his sister was behind everything since the rock-throwing incident.

Not more than a minute later, the clerk texted him back. *That's them. I'd remember that boy's contagious smile anywhere.*

With a heavy heart, Curt texted back his thanks.

"Your sister sent the flowers?" Annie asked by way of confirmation.

"Yes."

"Maybe she hadn't intended to scare me. The bouquet *was* lovely, and the sentiment could have been genuine."

"Maybe. But then why not take ownership for it after learning that it spooked you?" "Maybe she hoped they'd spook me into leaving town. Or she didn't want to admit that she'd scared me."

"At least I don't have to worry about you tonight. Because I don't plan to let her out of my sight until she knows this behavior has to end. Immediately."

"Wait." Annie nibbled her thumbnail. "Sylvie couldn't have been the guy in the hoodie. She was waiting for me at the community center when he followed me. And Bernie isn't spry enough for it to have been him."

Curt's brow furrowed. "Could you have been wrong about the guy following you? Sylvie might have seen it as an opportunity to play up your fears. Or been genuinely worried it was Joey, since that was before I told her he was dead."

Annie didn't appear convinced. "Then what about Ray's murder?"

Curt grimaced. "Sylvie isn't capable of murder."

"The note with today's flowers takes credit for the murder," Annie reminded him softly.

"She was bluffing to try to scare you away."

"Maybe, but do you think the county PD will see it that way?"

Pushing his fingers through his hair, Curt dropped his gaze. *Not given the note left at the scene they wouldn't.* "Bernie is good for the murder," he insisted. After all, what were the chances of a third person being out there, bent on tormenting her?

"Is there evidence to prove it?" Annie pressed. "Because a couple of days ago, you were sure Kai was responsible."

Curt winced. "I called that wrong." He couldn't fault her for questioning his judgment after all his sister put her through. "But I'm not wrong about my sister. She lives next door. I would've heard if she drove out the night Adams was killed."

Annie's soft blue eyes brimmed with empathy. "What are you going to do?"

Annie was the most remarkable woman he'd ever met. Why did his sister have to feel so threatened by her?

"Curt?" she prodded.

"I'm going to tell Sylvie I know everything, and see how she responds."

Curt found Sylvie in his kitchen, making supper.

"It's great to see you home so early." She lowered her voice and glanced around the kitchen doorway to where Noah was practicing yo-yo tricks. "Were you involved in that standoff outside of town? It was all over the radio."

"Yeah, we finally nabbed the guy who tried to kill Annie."

Sylvie went back to the vegetables she'd been chopping at the counter. "That's fabulous news," she said, but her tone didn't match her words. "I imagine she's relieved." Using the knife edge, Sylvie scraped the veggies from the chopping board into the frying pan, then washed her hands and wiped them on a towel. "Since you're home so early, I think I'll leave you to this and catch up on my bookkeeping."

Curt caught her arm. "Stay, please."

Her head tilted, her expression unreadable.

"I need to talk to you."

"What is it?" The question sounded more accusatory than worried, but Noah chose that moment to burst into the kitchen.

"Dad, you're home. Come see the new trick I can do."

Curt smiled at his son. "I'd love to." As he let his son lead him by the hand into the other room, Curt said over his shoulder to his sister, "Stay, please. We'll talk after Noah goes to bed."

Sylvie's gaze shifted to Noah, and her expression softened. "Of course."

Twenty minutes later, a delicious aroma filled the air. Freshly showered, Curt joined his sister in the kitchen again and gave her an affectionate shoulder squeeze. "Have I told you lately how much I appreciate you?" He smiled at Noah. "I hope you appreciate how much your aunt Sylvie spoils us."

Noah grinned. "She made me peanut butter cookies today too."

Sylvie gave Noah a hug. "How could I refuse when you asked so nicely?"

The meal passed with no hint of the tension she'd exuded earlier, even though Curt's insides were wound tighter than Noah's new yo-yo. She did the dishes while Curt kicked a soccer ball around with Noah outside, and then they both participated in the usual bedtime routine.

After listening to Noah's bedtime prayer, Curt silently added one of his own. *Lord, please show me how to interrogate my sister with love.*

Sylvie joined Curt in the living room, carrying two mugs of steaming coffee. "What did you need to talk about? Is the department changing your shift rotation again?"

"No, nothing like that." Curt took the mugs from Sylvie and set them on an end table, then clasped her hands and urged her to sit. "It's about what you've been doing."

She raised an eyebrow, feigning confusion, but the telltale tremble of her lips gave away her mental gymnastics. "What do you mean?"

"What you've been doing to Annie. I know about the card you wrote. The flowers." He hesitated, not wanting to assume too much, but wanting to push enough to convince her he already knew. "The rock throwing." He squeezed her hands. "Everything."

Sylvie burst into tears. Yanking her hands from his, she covered her face. "I don't know what came over me."

"You were hurt by the attention Noah showed her. And maybe worried about mine toward her too?" he pressed gently.

Sylvie peered at him through her fingers, likely a little stunned that he'd worked that out. "It was her stalker story. It resurrected all the horrible memories of my friend's experience. And when I saw how fond of her you were getting, I was terrified she'd bring that danger to our doorstep."

Curt gritted his teeth and strained to keep the irritation from his voice. "So terrified that you decided to scare her into believing her stalker had found her?"

"For all I knew, he had. I was trying to help her realize she'd be better off moving on sooner rather than later."

Curt sucked in a breath and held it. Despite the note found under Ray's body, Curt couldn't bring himself to accuse his sister of murder. "I realize how hurt you must have felt when Noah asked Annie to participate in activities that he normally did with you."

She snorted and brushed off the notion with a sweep of her hand. "That wasn't it at all. I was concerned about his safety."

"You don't need to be." Curt clasped her hand once more. "Annie's saboteur has been arrested. And Joey is dead. No one is coming after her. Or Noah. Or you." He added the last part under his breath. Sylvie had dropped out of college after her roommate's stalker incidents. She hadn't been the target, but she'd suffered mentally and emotionally. He'd long suspected the incident was what made Sylvie shy away from close relationships. He should have realized Annie's situation would resurrect all that buried fear.

Tears glistened in Sylvie's eyes.

Curt gave her hand an encouraging squeeze. "And I don't want you to have any doubt about how much we appreciate all you do for us, and how much we want you around. No matter what the future holds, you will always be part of our lives."

Relief softened her features. "I'm sorry for my childish behavior. I guess I should apologize to Annie."

Curt chuckled. "Yeah, but not with flowers."

Sylvie snagged her cup of coffee and leaned back on the sofa. Curt did the same, waiting to see if she'd divulge anything more. She didn't. She quickly drained her mug, staring every which way except at him. A moment later, she plunked it back on the coffee table. "I need to be off. I have correspondence to finish before I call it a night."

"I appreciate you staying so we could talk."

She pushed to her feet and reached for their mugs.

"Leave these. I'll clean up." Thankfully, she didn't seem to recognize his ulterior motive. After seeing her out, Curt bagged her mug so he could run the prints on it the next morning.

Because as much as he wanted to believe her, the cop in him couldn't let anyone off—not even his sister—without ensuring she was telling the truth.

21

The morning of the Founder's Day Picnic, Annie arrived at Grace's promptly at ten o'clock and carried her two massive coolers out to the car. "Are you sure you made enough?" Annie teased, her heart feeling lighter than it had in more than a week—more than a decade, really. Joey would never bother her again and her recent troubles were behind her. She could finally stop living in fear.

"Ian and Gayle are joining us," Grace said. "And of course, I wanted to have plenty of extra snacks on hand for any of the Sunday school children who stop by to say hi to their Grandma Grace."

Annie smiled, having no doubt one of the children would be Noah. Curt had asked if she planned to attend and had appeared pleased when said yes. But since he was on duty until four that afternoon, he'd suggested they might watch the fireworks together later.

Annie's stomach fluttered at the thought—not at the prospect of spending time with Curt so much as the prospect of seeing Sylvie for the first time since her mischief had been exposed. Although Annie had already forgiven Sylvie in her heart, the meeting was bound to be awkward. She'd refrained from telling Gayle and Ian that Sylvie had been responsible for anything, especially the rock throwing. But considering Gayle had suffered the brunt of Sylvie's irresponsible actions in that regard, Annie hoped Sylvie would apologize to her.

Annie loaded Grace's lawn chair into the trunk and then took the stack of picnic blankets she held. "Is that everything?"

Grace straightened her floppy-brimmed straw hat, then hitched her camera strap up her shoulder. "That's everything."

"Okay, then let's head out."

By the time they reached the park, cars lined both sides of the street for two blocks. "Wow, it looks as if the entire town is here," Annie said.

"It's a popular event. And the weather is perfect."

"I'll drop off you and the food near the pavilion, then find a parking spot," Annie offered.

"You're a dear."

Annie pulled up next to the pavilion and unloaded the chairs and cooler from her trunk while Grace collected her picnic basket.

"Hey, Ms. Bishop," Colin Mitchell called. "Can I give you and Grandma Grace a hand with those?"

Annie smiled at the teen, pleased to see their previous encounters hadn't caused him to shy away from her. "That would be great. I need to park the car, so perhaps you—"

"I can park your car for you," Colin volunteered.

"Nice try."

He shrugged, but a grin broke through the innocent expression he'd tried to hold.

"How about you tote Grace's cooler and lawn chair to wherever she'd like to sit?"

"No problem."

As Annie went to find parking along the road, she spotted Curt in an orange reflector vest, directing traffic. Stopping beside him, she rolled down her window. "So this is what they have Safe Haven's top crime fighters doing, is it?"

He touched the brim of his hat. "Yes ma'am. We don't get much trouble in these here parts." An eye-crinkling grin accompanied his silly drawl.

She giggled.

"I'm afraid I'm going to have to ask you to move along, ma'am. But"—he bent forward, bringing his face within inches of hers—"I can't wait to join you at tonight's fireworks."

At his wink, butterflies took flight in her stomach. Even in a reflector vest, he was incredibly handsome. She was still grinning when she finally found a parking spot three blocks away, and she didn't know what to make of the bubbly feeling in her chest. By not wanting to give Joey and his ilk any ammunition to leverage against her, she'd spent too many years distancing herself from any kind of emotional attachment.

And before Curt, she'd never considered that that might be a bad thing. But Joey was gone forever. And for the first time, she had the unsettling thought that, as content with life as she'd convinced herself she was over the past eight years, she hadn't really lived or loved.

More unsettling was her fear that she wasn't sure she knew how to truly love.

Resisting the temptation to stop and chat with Curt again, Annie cut through the grounds to get back to where she'd left Grace. But Colin had apparently already finished getting her settled elsewhere. Annie scanned the area and found herself shaking off the prickly sensation that she was being watched.

Noah jumped up and down, waving his arms. "We're over here."

Annie joined the pair, and Noah greeted her with a bear hug at hip height, almost bowling her over.

She laughed. "I'm happy to see you too. I saw your dad directing traffic. Where's your aunt?"

"She's manning a booth for her business. I'm hanging out with my friend until she's done with her shift and we can eat."

"In the meantime," Grace interjected, "I gave him a little something to tide him over."

Annie grinned at Noah's chocolate-smeared smile. "I never would have guessed."

"Come play some games with us." Noah motioned to a row of tents featuring various activities, from face painting to target practice.

Annie glanced toward Grace, who waved her on. "You go. I'll have plenty of company stopping by. Besides, Gayle and Ian will be here shortly."

"Are you sure?"

"Of course."

After trying their hands at several games and splitting a cone of cotton candy, Annie left Noah and his friend to jump in an inflatable castle and returned to Grace, who had been joined by Gayle and Ian.

"Hey," Gayle said. "I guess you finally got a good night's sleep now that your attacker is behind bars."

"I did sleep well." Annie sank into the lawn chair beside Gayle, opting not to mention Sylvie's role in the attacks.

"Have you browsed the vendors' booths yet?" Gayle asked.

"Not yet. Noah's been giving me a tour of the activity tents."

"He's such a sweet boy," Grace chimed in, her eyes twinkling with Annie had once heard her daughter-in-law call "a matchmaker's gleam."

Annie agreed, then averted her gaze to the vendors' booths, hoping to dissuade Grace from expanding on whatever notion was brewing in that hopelessly romantic mind of hers. "Anyone interested in wandering through the booths with me?"

"You and Gayle should," Grace said. "I'm content to sit here to watch and chat with passersby."

Gayle grabbed the cane she'd switched to after a couple of days on crutches. "I'm game."

They wandered through booths of homemade lotions and soaps, hand-knit sweaters and hand-sewn children's clothes, and others selling every imaginable kind of wood bauble. A booth displaying unique jewelry caught Gayle's attention, so Annie moved on to Sylvie's booth exhibiting her business's collection of shoe designs.

Sylvie acknowledged Annie with a nod, her expression tight.

Annie summoned a cheerful lilt. "How's business?"

"Good." Sylvie focused on straightening a row of shoes that wasn't crooked.

At her clipped response, Annie tried again. "Listen, Curt told me what you did. And I wanted to say that I understand where you were coming from, and I carry no hard feelings. I hope we can be friends."

"You know where I'm coming from?" Sylvie hissed. "You have no idea." She jutted her chin toward the activity tents. "I saw you playing with Noah, buying him cotton candy. If you really love him, you'll walk away."

Annie gaped at Sylvie, dumbfounded. "I don't understand."

Sylvie drew Annie behind the tent, out of view of shoppers, where the sound of the fast-flowing river muffled their voices. "They never found your stalker's body. He could still be out there." Sylvie curled her trembling hands into fists. "He could still come after you."

"That won't happen," Annie said softly, even as a whisper of fear twinged in her chest. Given the frenzy edging Sylvie's voice, she was clearly still rattled by her roommate's stalker experience and feared that not only would history repeat itself, but Noah would get caught in the crossfire. "Trust me. I would never let anyone hurt Noah."

"You better believe you won't." Sylvie's face reddened. "You should have gotten the message you're not wanted here when your CO detector went off."

Annie's eyes widened. "*You* stuffed my furnace pipe?"

"I was protecting Noah. If you died, the danger to him died with you."

The cold admission sent a chill through Annie's body. She stared into Sylvie's dark, angry eyes, and realized for the first time that the woman was capable of murder. "You wanted me dead?"

Sylvie snorted. "I knew your carbon monoxide detector would warn you before it was too late. But I hadn't counted on that squatter removing the batteries."

"That was you in the dark sedan when I ran out of the house." Sylvie smirked.

"Why kill Ray?" The words tore from Annie's throat. The man had died because of her, because she'd let herself fall in love with a little boy and his father.

Sylvie's eyes sparked, as if she enjoyed taunting Annie with her secrets. "I've raised Noah since he was a toddler. There's no way I'm going to stand by and let you endanger my nephew."

"I would never—"

"That's right. Never." She jabbed a finger into Annie's shoulder. "Got it?"

Annie stiffened, her shoulder stinging. "I can't leave them now."

"Oh, but you will."

"Aunt Sylvie, no!" Noah skidded up between them as Sylvie lashed out a second time.

Sylvie hit him instead of Annie. The boy staggered backward, and Sylvie's anger instantly became horror.

Noah lost his footing and tumbled into the river.

"Noah!" Sylvie shrieked.

Annie kicked off her shoes and plunged in after him.

Upriver, the hydroelectric dam's alarm sounded, warning of an imminent water discharge that could create dangerous currents.

Fear ripped through Annie's chest as she frantically searched the water.

Noah bobbed to the surface, arms flailing. He managed a single cry before he sank under the water again.

Annie powered toward him. She snagged the back of his shirt and struggled to pull his head above water.

A surge charged toward them. Her fingers squeezed tighter around Noah's collar. *Hang on. Please, God.* The prayer screamed through her mind as the explosive current swept them downriver. She clenched his shirt, but her fingers were numb with cold, and the water tore the fabric from her grasp.

She screamed.

Noah's pale face disappeared beneath the dark water.

$\mathcal{C}$urt spun around at a woman's shriek. It sounded like his sister. The dispatcher's voice came over the radio on Curt's shoulder—a boy in the river near the hydroelectric dam.

Noah? Curt sprinted across the parking lot and dodged the crowds on the grass.

The blare of approaching fire engines and ambulances sounded in the distance.

Curt ran faster than he'd believed possible. The boy couldn't be Noah. He'd repeatedly warned Noah of the dangerous undertows whenever the dam let loose.

The woman's shrieks grew louder. It was definitely Sylvie.

Curt's blood iced. "Police! Out of my way." He pushed through the gathering crowd. *Please, Lord, let Noah be okay.* He wouldn't have climbed the fence restricting access to the water. He wouldn't have. But even beyond the booms, the abrupt change in current could topple a canoe or catch a weak swimmer off guard.

"You've got to save him," Sylvie screamed to two men who'd dived in.

"Sylvie," Curt shouted, already kicking off his shoes as he crossed the remaining yards to the river's edge.

Sylvie spun around, her face white, tears streaking her cheeks. "It's Noah."

Curt unbuckled his duty belt, passed it to Sylvie for safekeeping, then raced along the shore, scanning the water for his son.

"There," someone called and pointed to a head that bobbed up to the surface.

Recognizing Annie, Curt dived into the river.

"Save Noah," Annie yelled when she saw him. "He's ahead of me."

Almost at her side, Curt faltered, his gaze clinging to hers—the woman who'd sacrifice her life for his son's.

"Go. I can make it out," she insisted.

A rescue line splashed into the water, and, entrusting her rescue to his fellow townsfolk, Curt surged forward in search of his son. *Please, God, let me find him in time.* He dived under and peered in every direction until his lungs burned. Seeing nothing, he kicked back to the surface. The sun had disappeared, blotted out by the clouds. *Please, Lord, I can't lose my son. Not him too.* Curt stroked downriver, his eyes stinging from the silt in the water.

"Got him." The shout rose from about twenty yards downriver, where a teen excitedly waved his arm above the water.

Curt swam toward them. Seconds before he reached them, a second teen helped the first hoist Noah, sputtering, to waiting arms on dry ground. Paramedics immediately began checking him over. One of the teens extended a hand to help Curt climb out of the river.

Tears welling in his eyes, Curt pulled the teen into a hug. "Thank you for saving my boy."

"It's the least we could do when you keep us all safe every day," the teen replied.

Curt sank to his knees beside Noah and clasped his hand. "I'm here, Noah."

One of the paramedics dropped a dry blanket over Curt's shoulders.

Noah stared at him with saucer-sized eyes. "Where's Annie? She didn't—" His voice hitched.

Curt glanced up to find Annie racing toward them with Grandma Grace and Ian and Gayle trailing in her wake. "She's fine."

Annie's strawberry-blonde hair was plastered to her head, her clothes dripped, and wild fear gleamed in her eyes. Yet she was still the most beautiful sight he'd seen next to his son's smiling face. "Noah? Are you okay?"

Curt jumped up and caught her in his arms. "He's fine. He's going to be fine." Emotions more powerful than the dam's water surge welled in his chest, and he buried his face in her shoulder. "Thank you."

Noah pushed to his feet and wrapped his arms around both of them.

Curt's palm skimmed her arm, her shoulder, before coming to rest on her cheek, still cool and damp from her plunge. "I didn't want to leave you, but I had to find him."

Her eyes misted, and she covered his hand with her own. "I know."

"I don't want to lose you."

Longing brimmed in her eyes, chased by a swell of sadness that gutted him. A tear slid down her cheek.

Curt whisked the tear away with a sweep of his thumb. "Don't cry. Everything will be fine." He scooped Noah into his arms and steered Annie toward his son's rescuers. "Attention, everyone." He spoke loud enough for the crowd to hear. "I'd like to thank everyone who helped save my son, and especially to our two heroes of the day who pulled him out of the water." Curt shook each of the teens' hands. "I owe you both a debt I'll never be able to repay."

Annie followed suit, then whispered teasingly to Curt. "I guess this means you'll have to rethink your view on teen hoodlums, huh?"

Curt huffed as he returned Noah to the waiting paramedics. "Yeah, I guess I will."

Annie pressed a kiss to the top of Noah's head. "And thank you for being my hero."

"Some hero *I* am." Noah seemed disappointed, tightening his grip on the blanket the paramedics had given him. "I fell into the river while trying to save you."

Curt stiffened. "Trying to save *you?*" he asked Annie. "From whom?" When she pressed her lips into a tight line, Curt's gaze snapped to Noah. "How did you fall into the river?"

"It was an accident. She was real mad, and I got in the way."

She? "Sylvie?" Curt scanned the crowd. *Where is she?* He refocused on Annie. "What happened?"

Annie winced. "I told her I didn't blame her and hoped we could be friends, but I think fear of being shut out of Noah's life is still blinding her."

"If she's in such bad shape that she's endangering Noah and still threatening you, that's exactly what *will* happen," he hissed.

Annie gripped his shoulder. "Hey, hey. You know your sister would never deliberately hurt Noah. She loves him more than anyone in the world."

"You're the one who jumped in to save him," Curt argued. "Risking your own life. *That's* true love."

Annie blinked repeatedly, as if straining to contain a rush of tears. "But your sister has been like a mother to him for most of his life. I can understand how she'd feel ripped apart at the prospect of being—"

"Replaced?" His heart thundered, even as he realized how much he wanted Annie in their lives.

Annie ducked her head, her voice suddenly quiet. "I think it's what she fears."

From the moment Curt met Annie, she'd stirred such intense emotions within him. Had Sylvie seen it long before he was ready to acknowledge what such feelings could mean?

"I think we'd better get the three of you home and into dry clothes,"

Grace interjected. "The paramedic says Noah is going to be fine. But we don't want all of you catching cold."

Ian handed Curt the shoes and vest he'd shed before jumping into the water. "Someone said these were yours."

"Yeah, thanks." Curt glanced around. "Have you seen Sylvie? I gave her my duty belt to hold."

"No, I haven't."

"I saw her hand it off to another officer." Grace's brow furrowed. "I assumed she was coming this way."

A chilling thought sliced through Curt's mind. What if Sylvie got it into her head that Noah hadn't made it out of the river alive?

His panic must have shown in his face because Annie clasped his arm. "What's wrong?"

"Grace, Gayle, can you stay with Noah? I have to find Sylvie."

"Of course," they agreed in unison.

Curt hugged Noah once more. "I'll be back as soon as I can," he promised. "Stay with Grandma Grace." Curt motioned Ian and Annie to where Noah wouldn't hear them. "We've got to find Sylvie." His voice cracked and he blinked hard. "If she doesn't know Noah survived, and blames herself . . ."

"I'll check the parking area," Ian said, taking off at a run.

Annie's eyes widened. "You can't think she'd—?"

"I don't know. I barely recognize her at this point." Curt ground his teeth so hard it was a wonder they didn't crack. "The Sylvie I know would be here checking on Noah." He squeezed the talk button on his radio receiver and ordered officers to be on the lookout for his sister, and gave a basic description.

"I'll check the restrooms," Annie said.

"Good idea." Curt hoped the explanation for Sylvie's absence was that simple. But nothing would have taken his sister away before she knew whether Noah was safe. As a cop, he'd seen that kind of thing before—a grieving parent blamed themself for their child's accident and saw no way to live with the guilt. Curt strode toward Sylvie's vendor booth, though he was certain her business would be the last thing on her mind.

An officer's voice sounded over the radio. "There's a woman on the tower."

"Sylvie?" Curt took off at a sprint.

"Hair color is right. I'm heading up. She doesn't seem too steady."

The instant he caught sight of her, Curt's breath stalled in his chest. Sylvie teetered at the safety rail of the forty-foot-high viewing platform. Curt caught hold of the officer starting up the stairs. "Let me go. That's my sister."

The cop allowed him to pass. "I'll watch your back."

Curt raced up the stairs. But when he reached the last steps, he slowed to a crawl, not wanting to spook her.

She stood on a bench seat she must've shoved closer to the guardrail. She spun around, stumbling precariously. "It's all my fault." Tears stained her face.

"He's okay, Sylvie. We got him." Curt slowly closed the distance between them. "Noah's fine. Just worried about you."

Her eyes unfocused, she wailed in a voice as wobbly as her legs, "I thought I'd be able to spot him from up here." She stepped back, bumping against the rail and clasping it in a white-knuckled grip.

He froze. It was clear she hadn't heard him. "Sylvie," he said firmly, to snap her out of her grief. "Noah is alive. We got him out."

Fresh tears trickled down her cheeks. "I love him so much. I would never do anything to hurt him."

Curt took another cautious step closer. "He knows that. We both do."

"I can't lose him."

The words, so similar to those of his prayer in the water, softened Curt's heart. "You haven't."

"He loves Annie." Sylvie sniffled. "He heard what I said to her. He'll hate me for it."

"No, he won't." Curt extended his hand toward her. "Let's go home." He couldn't see the ground below, but he imagined crowds had gathered there as they'd done along the river. Small-town folks had long memories. Curt and Sylvie did not need to have the discussion in public. "Come on, Sylvie. Noah wants to see you."

She buried her clenched fists under her armpits and dropped her gaze to her feet. "After what I did, I'll wind up in jail, and that will make all of this even worse for Noah." Her voice was flat, emotionless.

Curt felt as if a hand had reached inside his chest and wrenched out his heart. "Are you telling me you killed Ray Adams?"

Her head snapped up. "No. I could never."

"Then we can work this out, Sylvie. I don't think Annie will press charges for the mischief you caused. She wants to be friends."

Sylvie snorted, then lifted her face to the sky. "Monday night, when I saw you talking to her on the phone and smiling to yourself like she wasn't putting Noah in danger, I was so mad. I went for a walk to work off the steam. At some point, I passed Ray's place and noticed his van door standing open. That was how I knew it was his place—because his name was on the side of the van."

Curt couldn't breathe. What was Sylvie saying?

"When I passed by his place again twenty minutes later, the van door was still open. I figured he forgot to shut it when he came home, so I walked up the driveway and closed it. That's when I noticed the kitchen door standing open and him sprawled on the floor."

The breath Curt had been holding whooshed from his chest.

"I didn't have my cell phone on me and didn't see a house phone," Sylvie went on. "Not that it would've mattered because his body was already cold." Her voice hardened. "I ran home to tell you, but you were still on the phone with Annie. That's when I got the idea of leaving the note to make you think Joey killed Ray."

Curt groaned. From the corner of his eye, he caught sight of the other officer edging closer to Sylvie from the opposite direction.

Oblivious, Sylvie continued her story. "For all I knew, Annie's stalker did kill him. It was before you told me Joey was dead. So I wrote the note and ran back to Ray's house. I tucked it under the body, cleaned up the spilled soda I'd stepped in and tossed the cup in the garbage, then wiped my prints off everything I'd touched and got out of there. It's the truth." She dropped her hands to her sides. "You've got to believe me. I'm not a murderer." She noticed the other officer, and her eyes widened.

Curt motioned him to hold his position. "I do believe you." He caught her hand. "Now, let's go home."

"I can't face Noah." She jerked free of Curt's hold, and her momentum caused her to topple over the guardrail.

At Curt's soul-wrenching cry, Annie dashed up the last steps two at a time. He sank to his knees, hands sliding down the wrought iron fence surrounding the deck, as the other officer murmured condolences.

Annie's heart broke at the sight of Curt's shuddering shoulders, the sound of his anguished sobs. Apparently, neither man had the stomach to peek over the side to the ground below. Annie rushed to Curt as applause erupted below, assuring her the plan had worked. She glanced over the edge, then drew him to his feet. "Curt, she's okay."

Hollowed-out eyes met hers. "I should've saved her."

Annie hugged him with all her might. "You did."

Behind them, the other officer's gasp told her that he'd realized what had happened. He moved away.

Annie turned Curt to the safety rail and urged him to look down.

He resisted. "What am I going to do without her?"

"Fortunately, you don't have to find out. She's safe," Annie repeated, and the words finally seemed to penetrate the haze of his grief.

Curt peered over the rail. His eyes widened at the sight of a pair of firefighters helping Sylvie out of the open-roofed inflatable castle. "How?" Curt asked.

"It was Colin's idea. We were afraid she might jump. While I ran Colin's idea past the firefighters, he recruited his friends to help move the inflatable castle into position beneath where she stood. And you kept her talking long enough for us to get it there in time."

Curt clung to Annie. "Thank you."

"It wasn't me. It was the boys."

Curt pulled back. "I owe them a huge apology for my attitude toward them. For all the grief they've given our department lately with their mischief, they sure came through when it counts."

Annie clasped his hand. "No time like the present. And I'm sure your sister will need you now more than ever."

Curt squeezed Annie's hand as they descended the stairs together. "Your love astounds me."

Her foot missed the next step, and she would've fallen if not for Curt's firm hold on her. *Love?* "I don't know what you mean."

His broad smile crinkled the corners of his eyes. "You really don't, do you? You do it as if it's the most natural thing on earth."

"Loving?"

He chuckled. "Yes. The Bible says, 'Love is patient. Love is kind.

It does not envy. It does not boast . . . It keeps no record of wrongs. It does not delight in evil, but rejoices in the truth. It always protects, always trusts, always hopes, always perseveres.' And that's exactly how you've treated us since we met." His gaze dropped to their entwined fingers. "I think that's what most attracted me to you from the first day we met."

She froze.

He skimmed his thumb over her bottom lip, and only then did she realize she was staring at him, mouth agape. "You are the most caring person I know."

She blinked. He must be confusing her with someone else.

"Despite all the horrible things my sister did to try to scare you away, you've shown her nothing but kindness. You've championed her to both Noah and me. You are truly remarkable. And I think I've fallen in love with you."

Her heart swelled so joyously she could've floated the remaining two stories to the ground. "You love me?" she whispered.

He framed her face in his hands and brushed his lips against hers. Every cell in her being strained toward him. She wrapped her arms around his waist and leaned into the kiss.

Joy and peace swirled within her. She finally understood what love was—and how it felt for dreams to come true.

Epilogue

Two months later

When Annie arrived at Grace's for Thanksgiving dinner, Sylvie greeted her at the door. "I'm so glad you could join our celebration." Sylvie drew her into the living room.

Annie's heart warmed at the sight of Kai, who gave her a friendly wave from where he sat on a sofa. She smiled and waved back at the young man, who appeared healthy and comfortable in Grace's home. Annie was glad that Kai and Grace seemed to have mended fences after all that had happened.

"Did Curt tell you?" Sylvie asked.

"Tell me what?"

"I've been officially exonerated from having anything to do with Ray's death."

Annie whooped and gave Sylvie a warm hug.

Sylvie hugged her back. She appeared to be doing well since her brief stint at a mental health care facility and continued counseling appointments, and the news had clearly lifted a dark cloud from her shoulders.

Curt carried a large platter into the dining room table, visible from where Annie and Sylvie stood. He gave Kai a friendly nod before speaking to Annie. "She told you?"

"Yes," Annie exclaimed. "It's great news."

"The forensics evidence from Ray's house proved that a cup of soda spilled on Ray's clothes and on the floor where he fell, corroborating

Sylvie's story. That, plus her fingerprints on his van door, and the takeout receipt in his truck—time-stamped ten minutes before the estimated time of his death—and I was confident clearing her was a mere formality."

"But do they know how Ray died?" Annie asked softly.

Curt's voice was full of sorrow. "The coroner believes that poor Ray choked on an ice cube and hit his head on the counter as he fell."

Sylvie squeezed Annie's arm. "Your statement went a long way in convincing the prosecutor not to press charges against me for obstructing their investigation. After how horrible I behaved toward you, I wouldn't have blamed you for wanting me locked up."

Grace bustled in carrying a steaming bowl of mashed potatoes. "Everyone understands that you were hurting, Sylvie. You needed help, not censure."

Annie agreed, grateful Gayle and Ian had felt the same when Sylvie asked for their forgiveness for throwing rocks at them. It had taken a few weeks of counseling, but by the time she owned up to everything she'd done, Sylvie was genuinely remorseful. She had even admitted to hiring a teen in a hoodie to follow Annie to the community center so that she could appear horrified.

Curt sidled over to Annie and wrapped his arm around her. "Don't worry, Sylv, you can make up the community service you should have gotten for your other stunts by babysitting for us."

He planted a kiss on Annie's cheek that set her heart thrumming. But Annie worried Sylvie wouldn't appreciate her brother's teasing, since Grace, Annie, and even Colin Mitchell, had taken over her role in caregiving for Noah since the incident at the park.

"Call on me anytime." Sylvie playfully smacked her brother's shoulder, not appearing at all distressed by his teasing. "As much as I cherished co-parenting Noah with you, I'm looking forward to being the doting aunt who can spoil him rotten and leave the fallout to you two."

Annie's heart jumped at Sylvie's presumption—equating her with Curt as Noah's guardian. She gazed out the window to where Noah and Colin kicked a soccer ball around outside. After a decade of hiding and resisting close relationships, she was ready to embrace being part of a wonderful family.

"Did Curt tell you he got Colin a job as an assistant coach for the indoor soccer season?" Sylvie asked.

"No." Annie tilted her head and eyed him with curiosity.

Curt shrugged. "The team had an opening, and I told the head coach what a great kid Colin is."

"That's high praise coming from you," Sylvie teased.

Curt rolled his eyes. "I figured having something constructive to do after school would keep the kid out of mischief."

Annie reined in a smirk, pretty sure the glowing recommendation had more to do with Curt's gratitude toward Colin for saving Sylvie's life.

Colin headed off down the street, and Noah raced inside, his soccer ball tucked under his arm. "Did you ask her yet, Dad?"

Everyone chuckled but Annie, who suddenly had the feeling they all knew something she didn't.

Grace clapped her hands together. "No time like the present, I always say."

The blush that bloomed on Curt's cheeks kicked Annie's pulse into overdrive.

"Noah has been teaching Bella a new trick he'd like to show you." Curt motioned Noah to join him, then reached for Annie's hand. "But first, we'd like to ask you a question." His fingers trembled as they gently wrapped around hers. Annie struggled to breathe at the love shining in his eyes.

"You've brought such joy into our lives, and emotions I didn't think I'd ever feel again." Curt's voice cracked and he ducked his head.

Annie squeezed his hand encouragingly.

"I want you to be my mom," Noah blurted, apparently deciding his dad was taking too long to get to the point.

Moisture clung to Curt's eyelashes as his gaze found Annie's once more. "So much for the eloquent speech." He chuckled nervously. "What I was trying to say is that we love you and we want you to be part of our family."

Annie's heart threatened to burst with joy.

"We're a package deal," Noah stage-whispered to Ian.

Pressing her lips together, Annie couldn't resist teasing Curt. "Is there a question in there?"

He dropped her hand and patted his thigh. "Bella, come here, girl."

To Annie's surprise, Bella trotted into the room.

"Sit," Curt ordered. The dog obeyed, and Curt handed something to Noah before claiming Annie's hand once more and dropping to one knee beside Bella and his son.

"Bella, hold." Noah carefully balanced a delicate cluster diamond ring on Bella's nose, then grinned at Annie. "I think it's a yes, Dad."

"It is," Annie whispered.

"I still have to ask." Curt stroked his thumb across her hand, sending a ripple through her. "We're far from perfect, but we're better people with you in our lives, and we love you more than words can express. Would you do us the honor of marrying us?"

Annie flung herself into his arms. "Nothing would make me happier."

Curt cradled her face in his hands and sealed their promise with the tenderest kiss.

Bella poked her nose between them, the engagement ring still dutifully balanced on top. They laughed as Curt slipped the ring onto Annie's finger.

Grace snapped a photo with her camera. "Proof that a dog is never too old to learn a new trick."

Curt winked at Annie. "And neither are we. Right?"

She grinned back at him through happy tears. "So right."